JUM

"Well?" Lisa ... ns squawking as ...

Exedore turne... ...an ships, Admiral, I can assure you."

"Enhancement coming in now, Lisa," Rick said. The computer drew several clamlike shapes on the screen.

Breetai straightened up and grunted. "Invid troop carriers!"

"Could they have formed an alliance with the Masters?" Lisa asked.

"That is very unlikely, Admiral," Exedore answered her.

"Sir!" a tech shouted. "It's showing multiple paint through the field!" The clam-ships had opened, yawned, spilling forth an enormous number of small strike mecha.

"I want the Skull scrambled."

"General Edwards's Ghost Squadron is already out, sir," Blake reported from his duty station.

"What?!"

The threat board showed two clusters of blips closing on one another. Rick slapped his hand down on the com stud, demanding to know who ordered the Alpha Veritechs out.

"General Edwards," came the reply.

"Edwards!" Rick seethed.

Blake tapped in a rapid sequence of requests. "Sir. Ghost Squadron reports they're moving in to engage."

Published by Ballantine Books:

The ROBOTECH ™ Series

GENESIS #1

BATTLE CRY #2

HOMECOMING #3

BATTLEHYMN #4

FORCE OF ARMS #5

DOOMSDAY #6

SOUTHERN CROSS #7

METAL FIRE #8

THE FINAL NIGHTMARE #9

INVID INVASION #10

METAMORPHOSIS #11

SYMPHONY OF LIGHT #12

The SENTINELS ™ Series

THE DEVIL'S HAND #1

THE SENTINELS ™ #1
THE DEVIL'S HAND

Jack McKinney

3 9075 05439226 8

A Del Rey Book

BALLANTINE BOOKS • NEW YORK

A Del Rey Book
Published by Ballantine Books

Copyright © 1987, 1988 by HARMONY GOLD U.S.A., INC. and TAT-SUNOKO PRODUCTION CO. LTD. All Rights Reserved. ROBOTECH is a trademark owned and licensed by HARMONY GOLD U.S.A., INC.

All rights reserved under International and Pan-American Copyright Conventions. Published in the United States of America by Ballantine Books, a division of Random House, Inc., New York, and simultaneously in Canada by Random House of Canada Limited, Toronto.

Library of Congress Catalog Card Number: 87-91376

ISBN 0-345-35300-5

Manufactured in the United States of America

First Edition: April 1988

FOR NICHOLAS, JEREMY AND MATTHEW
WHOSE ENTHUSIASM HAS BEEN A
CONTINUING SOURCE OF INSPIRATION.

ROBOTECH CHRONOLOGY

1999   Alien spacecraft known as SDF-1 crashlands on Earth through an opening in hyperspace, effectively ending almost a decade of Global Civil War.

        In another part of the Galaxy, Zor is killed during a Flower of Life seeding attempt.

2002   Destruction of Mars Base Sara.

2009   On the SDF-1's launch day, the Zentraedi (after a ten-year search for the fortress) appear and lay waste to Macross Island. The SDF-1 makes an accidental jump to Pluto.

2009–11 The SDF-1 battles its way back to Earth.

2011–12 The SDF-1 spends almost half a year on Earth, is ordered to leave, and defeats Dolza's armada, which has laid waste to much of the planet.

2012–14 A two-year period of reconstruction begins.

2012   The Robotech Masters lose confidence in the ability of their giant warriors to recapture the SDF-1, and begin a mass pilgrimage through interstellar space to Earth.

2013   Dana Sterling is born.

2014   Destruction of the SDFs 1 and 2 and Khyron's battlecruiser.

2014–20 The SDF-3 is built and launched. Rick Hunter turns 29 in 2020; Dana turns 7.

Subsequent events covering the Tiresian campaign are recounted in the Sentinels series. A complete Robochronology will appear in the fifth and final volume.

CHAPTER
ONE

*I leave it up to the historians and the moralists to judge
whether our decision (the Expeditionary mission) is right or
wrong. I know only that it is prudent and necessary—necessary
for our very survival both as a planet and as a life-form. If the
Protoculture has taught me anything, it is that one must simply
act! When all is said and done the inevitabilities and reshapings
will have their way, but to remain either complacent or inert in the
face of those fatalities is to invite catastrophe of a higher order
than any of us dare imagine.*

From the personal journal of Dr. Emil Lang

IN THE MIDDLE OF THE NIGHT, ON AN ALIEN WORLD, AN
army of insentient warriors dropped from the sky. Tirol, as
this small moon was known, represented a prize of sorts—
the end of a long campaign that had taken the invaders
through a dozen local star systems and across the varied
faces of twice that number of worlds—the remote realms
of the once great empire of the Robotech Masters, forged
and secured by their giant soldier clones, the Zentraedi.
But Tirol itself was all but deserted, abandoned almost a
generation earlier by those same Masters. So in effect this
conquest was something of a disappointment for the horde
who had raised savagery to new heights, something of a
nonevent.

But just as a rock tossed into a pond will make its presence known to distant shores, the Invid's arrival on Tirol would send powerful waves through the continuum; and nowhere would the effects of their invasion be more greatly felt than on the world already inundated by previous tides from this same quarter—a blue-white gem of a planet that had seen better days, but was struggling still to regain control of its own fragile destiny. . .

Earth had captured its second satellite in the year 2013, when a joint Terran and XT force had wrested it from the control of the Zentraedi commander, Reno, faithful to the Imperative even after Dolza's fiery demise. The factory satellite was an enormous monstrosity, well in keeping with the grotesque design of the Zentraedi fleet, that had been folded instantaneously through space-time by Protoculture-fueled Reflex drives. It was radish-shaped and rose-colored in starlight, with fissures and convolutions suggestive of cerebral matter. Attached along its median section by rigid stalklike transport tubes were half a dozen secondary sacs and appendages, smaller by far, but equally vegetal in aspect, veined and incomprehensible.

There were some 15,000 Humans and Zentraedi living onboard, a sizable portion of Earth's post-apocalyptic population. The majority of these men and women had labored for six years inside the factory's weightless belly to construct a starship, a dimensional fortress soon to be Tirol-bound—there to confront the Robotech Masters, and with luck curtail any threat of continued warfare.

Among those onboard were Vice Admiral Rick Hunter and his close friend and trusted commander, Max Sterling. From a viewport in the admiral's quarters, the two men were watching null-gee construction crews put the finishing touches on the massive ship's deliberately misleading superstructure.

"I just don't know whether we're ready for this," Rick was saying. He had turned from the viewport and was three strides toward the center of the room. "There are so many *variables*, so many things that could go wrong now."

Max followed him, a grin beneath the sympathetic look he had adopted. "Come on, what could go wrong?"

Rick whirled on him. "Maybe I'm just not *ready*, Max!"

Rick's voice cracked on the word and Max couldn't suppress a short laugh. "Ready? It's been six years, Rick. How much more ready can you expect to be?"

"Guess I'm not as good up against the unknowns anymore." Rick shrugged, lowering his gaze. "I mean, we've got something good going already. So why jeopardize it, why tamper with it?"

Max took his friend by the shoulders and gave him an affectionate shake. "Look, you and Lisa love each other, so quit worrying. Everything's going to turn out fine. Besides, everybody's excited about the wedding. And what are you going to do, walk out on ten thousand guests?"

Rick felt the wisdom of it sink in, and smiled, self-mockingly.

They had both aged well, the rigors of life on- and off-world notwithstanding; both had turned twenty-nine in March and had at least a few good years left in them. Rick stood taller and straighter now than he had during the war, and that combined with some added weight gave him a stronger, more capable look. This was enhanced by the cut of the Expeditionary Force's high-collared uniform and torso harness, a crisscross, tailed, and flare-shouldered affair of black leather worn over tight-fitting trousers. He still wore his black hair stylishly long, though—a fashion the Veritech flyboys of the Robotech Defense Force had been largely responsible for. Max, too, had left behind the innocent look that had been something of a trademark. While Rick, Dr. Lang, and Lisa Hayes had devoted themselves to the SDF-3 project, Max had been busy distinguishing himself in the Southlands, especially during the Malcontent Uprisings of 2015–18. He still favored the blue hair tint he had affected during the war, likewise oversize aviator glasses to contacts or corrective microsurgery. Less than perfect vision had never handicapped his flying skills, in any case.

Rick was glancing back at the SDF-3 now. "And everybody gets to ride in the limo." He smirked.

Fabricated from the hull and power drives of Breetai's dreadnought and the salvaged remains from the SDFs 1 and 2, the ship was itself a wedding of sorts. Pursuant to Lang and Exedore's requests, it was more Zentraedi than Terran in design: a nontransformable deepspace leviathan, bristling with antennae and blistered across its crimson surface with scanner ports and laser-array gun turrets.

"We'll make sure you two get the backseat," Max said. "For at least a couple of hours, anyway."

Rick laughed from across the room; Max joined him at the external viewport, Earth's incomparable beauty filling the view. Sunlight glinted off the alloyed hulls and fins of dozens of in-transit shuttles. Rick was staring down at the planet wistfully.

"When's Lisa due back?" Max asked him.

"Tomorrow. But I'm thinking of shuttling down to meet her."

Max made an approving sound. "I'll ride with you."

"When haven't you," Rick said, after a moment.

With the destruction of the SDFs 1 and 2 on that fateful winter night in 2014, Macross's sister city, Monument, had risen to the fore as Earth's unofficial capital. The irradiated remains of Macross had been bulldozed flat and pushed into what hadn't been boiled away from Lake Gloval. Three enormous manmade buttes marked the resting place of the superdimensional fortresses, along with that of the Zentraedi cruiser that had destroyed them. But those mounds had not been completed before volunteer teams of valiant Robotechnicians had braved slow death to salvage what they could from the devastation.

Thrice-born Macross, however, was not resurrected, as much by choice as anything else; but the name lived on in a kind of mythic way, and Monument City, to the southwest over a rugged ridge, was doing its best to carry the tradition forward. This would change after the SDF-3 departed, but in 2020 things were much as they were in the Macross of 2014. That is not to say that there weren't sinister currents in the air for one and all to perceive; but the Expeditionary mission to Tirol was foremost on the minds of those who could have prevented the subsequent slide.

Monument was the seat of the United Earth Government, but the most important building in that burgeoning city was the headquarters of the newly-formed Army of the Southern Cross, a politico-military party that had its origins in the Southlands during the Malcontent Uprisings, and had all but superseded the authority formerly enjoyed by RDF, most of which was slated for the Expeditionary mission. The headquarters was a soaring megacomplex whose central tower cluster had been built to suggest the white gonfalons, or ensigns, of a holy crusade hanging from high crosspieces. The high-tech needles were crowned with crenels and merlons, like some medieval battlement, announcing to all the world the ideals and *esprit* of the Army of the Southern Cross.

Just now the building was host to a final press conference held jointly by members of the Expeditionary Mission Plenipotentiary Council, the RDF, and the Southern Cross. Dr. Emil Lang and the Zentraedi Ambassador, Exedore, spoke on behalf of the twelve-person council, while the military factions were represented respectively by Brigadier General Gunther Reinhardt and Field Marshal Anatole Leonard. The press was there in force, crowding the hall, jostling one another for position, snapping off shot after stroboscopic shot, and grilling the four-member panel with an overwhelming array of questions from special-interest groups and insulated power bases as distant as Cavern City and Brasilia in the Southlands.

Lang was doing his best to respond to one of these; for the third time, someone in the press corps had returned to the issue of Earth's potential vulnerability in the wake of the SDF-3's departure. As the high priest of Robotechnology, Lang had little interest in such mundane concerns, but he was doing his best to restate the importance of the mission and repeat launch details that had already been covered in the press releases.

"Final selections for the crew are proceeding and we should have no trouble meeting our launch schedule. If we are to avoid a second Robotech War, we must make peaceful contact with the Robotech Masters and establish a relationship of mutual cooperation. That is the mission of the SDF-3."

Murmurs of discontent spread through the crowd, and several reporters hurled insults of one sort or another. But then, could anyone expect anything in the way of a concrete response from someone like Lang? When the man chose to be profound, there were perhaps only a handful of scientists on Earth who could follow him. The rest of the time he came across as alien as any Zentraedi. Rumors and speculations about Lang went as far back as the early days on Macross Island, when he and Gloval, Fokker, Edwards, and a few others had first reconned the SDF-1, known then as "the Visitor." He had taken a Zentraedi mind-boost, some claimed, a megadose of Protoculture that had somehow integrated his internal circuitry with that of the ship itself. Certainly his marblelike eyes lent credence to the tale. Although he had been more visible, more accessible these past few years, he was still the same ethereal man who had been the driving force behind Robotechnology since the turn of the century.

"I want to take this opportunity to reemphasize that the Robotech Expeditionary Force is intended as a diplomatic mission," Exedore added without being asked. "The SDF-3 will be traveling to the homeworld of the Robotech Masters, the third moon of the planet Fantoma, known as Tirol." The Zentraedi motioned to the huge projection screen behind the speakers' platform, which showed a color schematic of the ringed giant's extensive system.

"The Masters themselves have not engaged in actual combat for nearly six generations. However, it is impossible to predict with certainty how they will react to our mission. For that reason the SDF-3 has been outfitted with a considerable arsenal of Robotech weaponry. In the event that we are met with force, we shall be ready and able to defend ourselves. But I must press the point that the departure of the fortress will not leave the Earth undefended. Commander Leonard and his staff have all the capabilities for defense necessary to repel any invasion force. And as the planet is not presently threatened by any enemy, we feel confident that the Earth is in no jeopard—"

"If I may interrupt for a moment," Leonard said angrily, getting to his feet. He had been biting back his words for half the press conference, but had reached his breaking point when Exedore—the *alien!*—began to imply that the

SDF-3 would be facing greater potential danger than abandoned Earth. Reporters throughout the hall—certainly those who had been planted there by the Southern Cross command to steer the conference toward this very confrontation—took advantage of the moment to get shots of the bearish, shaved-skulled field marshal confronting and towering over the XT ambassador. Leonard's hatred of the Zentraedi was no secret among the general staff. He had never met Exedore full-size, as it were, but perhaps detested him even more in his Micronized state, especially since Terran cosmologists had gone to work on him, styling his hair with a widow's peak, and concealing the clone's dwarfish anatomy beneath specially-tailored uniforms. Leonard often wished that Exedore had been among the Zentraedi Malcontents he had hunted down in the Southlands. . . .

"I'm not as optimistic as the *ambassador* about the lack of an enemy threat," Leonard continued, his face red with rage. "Mark my words, the departure of the SDF-3 and its weapons systems will leave the Earth hopelessly vulnerable to attack! Even that factory satellite's going to be nothing but a useless shell when the Expeditionary Force leaves. They've stripped it clean—and you've stripped us clean!"

"Gentlemen, please," Lang tried to interject, stretching his arms out between the two of them. Reinhardt, with his bald pate, beard, and fringe of premature gray hair, leaned back in his chair, overshadowed by Leonard's bulk.

"It's all very easy for him to say we'll be safe," the field marshal ranted. "When the attack comes, *he'll* be on the other side of the galaxy!"

"Frankly, I think you're a bit paranoid, Commander," Exedore announced evenly, almost clinically. "What attack do you mean—by whom, from where?"

Leonard's great jowls quivered; his eyes flashed a

hatred even Exedore couldn't help but feel. "For all we know, there could be a fleet of your fellow Zentraedi out there just waiting for us to drop our guard!"

"That will be enough, Commander Leonard," Reinhardt said at last. "Alarmist talk is of no use to anyone at this point."

Leonard swallowed the rebuke as flashes strobed without pause. He was aware that his position with the general staff was still somewhat tenuous; and besides, he had made his point.

"Gentlemen, you're cutting our defenses to almost nothing," he concluded, as shouts filled the hall. "Once the SDF leaves orbit I won't be able to defend the Earth against a flock of pigeons."

The press conference was being carried live around the world, and to Luna Base, Space Station Liberty, and the factory satellite. But where many were finding cause for concern in Leonard's contentions, there was one viewer aboard the satellite who merely laughed it off. He had a drink in hand, his feet crossed on the top of the monitor in his spacious quarters.

Leonard was overplaying the role, Major General T. R. Edwards told himself as he set the drink aside. But his performance would have the desired effect nonetheless.

Edwards knew even then that the Southern Cross would eventually gain the upper hand. If necessary, Professor Lazlo Zand would see to that. And Senator Moran, whom they had spent years grooming for high office, would ascend to the seat reserved for him.

Edwards fingered the ugly raised scars that coursed across the right side of his forehead and face—diagonally, from his hairline to the bridge of his nose, and from there in a reverse angle to the heel of his jawbone. The eye at the apex of this triangular disfiguration was dead, sewn shut to a dark slash. He would not be around to reap the immediate rewards of these complex conspiracies and manipulations, but all that could wait until his return from Tirol. First, there were scores to settle with older adversaries, scores that went back more than twenty years.

Not far from the Southern Cross headquarters in one of Monument City's more upscale shopping districts, Admiral Lisa Hayes was being fitted for her wedding gown. She had chosen one her late father would have approved of; it had a traditional, almost antebellum look, lots of satin, lace, and tulle, with a full, two-petticoat tiered skirt, long sleeves, and a simple round neck. The veil was rather short in contrast, with baby's breath and two silk roses affixed to the headband. Lisa gave an appreciative nod as the two fitters fell back smiling, allowing her center place in the shop's mirrored wall. She ran her fingers under the flip of her shoulder-length auburn hair—still unaccustomed to the cut—and said, "Perfect."

In the front room, Dr. Jean Grant and Captain Miriya Sterling wondered aloud what was taking Lisa so long, not out of concern but anticipation. The day was something of a shopping spree for Jean and Miriya as well; in less than a week they would be on their way to Tirol, and on this trip out the SDF wouldn't be traveling with a full city in its belly. *And who knows what to expect in the way of shops on Tirol*, Max had quipped when the two women left the factory satellite. They had brought the kids along, Dana and Bowie, both nearing eight years old, presently bored and antagonistic.

Bowie had Jean's petiteness and dark honey complexion; his health had never been robust, but that didn't prevent blond and lanky Dana from teasing him whenever she could. He was standing sullen-faced in the shop's doorway when she snuck up behind him to yank his SDF cap down over his face.

"Hey, cut it out!" Bowie yelled. "Why'd you do that, Dana?"

She returned a wide-eyed look of innocence, elaborate concern in her voice. "I didn't do anything. I think your brain must be getting smaller."

"Ahhh, *whose* brain's getting smaller?" Bowie said, working the visored cap up to where it belonged.

"Okay, I admit it, I'm guilty," Dana answered him, sincere all of a sudden. "I guess I can't pull the wool over *your* eyes."

Jean and Miriya had both turned at the sound of Bowie's initial howl, but they had long ago decided on a policy of nonintervention when it came to the kids. Though children were included in the Expeditionary mission, Bowie and Dana would not be among them. In Bowie's case it was a matter of health—a fact that had since steered Jean into research medicine. But Dana was exempt for reasons less clear-cut; as the only child of a Human-Zentraedi union, she had been studied, tested, and evaluated since birth, and was judged too precious a commodity to risk on such an enterprise. This, in any case, was the thinking of Professor Zand, who had headed up the medical teams, and Max and Miriya had reluctantly accepted the logic of it. The decision was unalterable now, no matter what, and it was guaranteed that Bowie and Dana would grow up as near siblings under the care of the Sterlings' close friends, Rolf and Laura Emerson.

Miriya was thinking these things through while she watched the children's bickering escalate, then dissolve into playful banter. "Look at them, Jean," she said the way only a mother can. "Do you think we're doing the right thing?"

Jean gave one of the clothes racks a casual spin. "Of course we are, sweetie. You know that."

The two women showed strained smiles to one another. How often they had talked about the irony of their friendship; how often they had remembered Jean's sister-in-law, Claudia Grant, who died in Khyron's suicide run against the SDF-1. And perhaps the conversation would have taken a turn in this direction even then, had not Lisa chosen just that moment to present herself as bride-to-be.

"Well, what do you think?" she asked them, turning around for their inspection.

Miriya, who had worn her hair emerald green for years, was too surprised by the gown's conservative cut to say much; but Jean said, "I think you picked a beauty, Admiral. That gown is shipshape from stem to stern."

"Yeah, but how will it travel in hyperspace?" Miriya thought to ask.

"You two . . ." Lisa laughed, while her friends began to finger the gown here and there. None of them were aware that a newcomer had entered the ship until a female voice said, "Excuse me."

Lisa looked up and uttered a surprised gasp. Lynn-Minmei was standing in the doorway. Lisa had been thinking of her not five minutes before, standing in front of the mirror seeing new age lines in her thirty-five-year-old face and comparing herself to the seemingly ageless star of song and screen.

"I—I hope I'm not interrupting, Lisa, but I heard you were in town, and well, I just wanted to congratulate you before the wedding. I mean, it's going to be such a madhouse up there." They had hardly been strangers these past six years, but hadn't seen each other since the wedding date had been officially announced some five months ago. "I'd love to help out any way I can—that is, if you'd allow me to, Lisa."

"Minmei," Lisa said with a note of disbelief. "This is so unexpected. But don't be silly, of course you can help," she added, laughing. "Come here."

They embraced, and held hands as they stepped back to regard one another. Lisa couldn't help but marvel at Minmei's youth and radiance. She really was the one constant in everyone's lives.

"Oh, Lisa, I want so much to let bygones be bygones. That dress is lovely—I always knew you'd make a beautiful bride."

"Ms. Minmei's right, Admiral," enthused the shop owner, who had appeared out of nowhere. It was obvious that the man was thrilled to have a celebrity of Minmei's stature in his boutique; he risked a glance at the street, hoping some passersby had noticed her enter.

"I still think she should get married in her EVA suit," Bowie said from across the room, only to have Dana pull the cap down on his forehead again.

"Children!" Jean scolded as the bickering recommenced.

Minmei asked to see the engagement ring, and Lisa held out her hand.

"I can't tell you what it means to see you again, Minmei," Lisa said softly.

"That devious little Zentraedi's got the whole Supreme Council eating out of his hand!" Commander Leonard complained to Rolf Emerson after the press conference.

Emerson, soon to inherit two eight-year-olds, was every bit the commander's opposite, in appearance as well as ideology; but the two of them had nevertheless managed to maintain a working relationship. Major Emerson, handsome, clean-cut, and fine-featured, was, strictly speaking, RDF; but he had become something of a liaison officer between the general staffs of the military factions. Well aware of Leonard's xenophobia—and of the infamous "thigh wound" the field marshal had sustained during the Malcontent Uprisings—Emerson was willing to let the racial slur slide, even though he numbered several Zentraedi among his closest and dearest friends.

"It's unbelievable," Leonard was railing, the huge brass buckle of his uniform dazzling even in the dim light of Emerson's headquarters office. "A diplomatic mission . . . If it's a *diplomatic* mission, then why are they arming that ship with every Robotech weapons system we've ever developed?"

"It's called 'gunboat diplomacy,' Commander," Emerson replied, willing to concede the point. Lord Exedore and Breetai claimed that they had no real knowledge of what the Robotech Masters might possess in the way of a war machine now that their race of warrior giants had all but been erased from the galaxy.

"Well, stupidity's what I call it. It jeopardizes the very survival of this planet." Leonard paced in front of Emerson's desk. "Something stinks here, Major, and it's not in the ventilation system."

TWO

In the midst of all the ironies and reversals, the struggles, treachery, conquests, and betrayals, the mad scramble for mutated Flowers and irradiated worlds, it was easy to lose sight of the war's central concern—which was not, as many have claimed, the Flowers of Life, but their deified stepchild, Protoculture. Even the Regis seemed to forget for a time; but it could hardly be said that the Regent's Invid, the Masters, or the Expeditionary mission, had anything other than Protoculture as their goal and grail. Protoculture was needed to fuel their mecha, to drive their war machines to greater and greater heights. And it was all but disappeared from the galaxy. What a trick it played on all of us!

Selig Kahler, *The Tirolian Campaign*

As it would happen, Commander Leonard's fears were justified, but eleven years would pass before the spade fortresses of the Robotech Masters appeared in Earthspace. And perhaps history would have vindicated Leonard if the man's misdeeds had not stayed one step ahead of his contributions. Fate offered him one consolation, though: he would be dead two years before the Invid arrival. Earth would fall, just as he had predicted; just as Tirol fell after the Masters had begun *their* long journey through space and left their homeworld defenseless.

The Invid, however, were less confident in those days. Optera—their native planet—and Tirol had been at war for generations, and the Invid especially were at a disadvantage in terms of firepower. They had, after all, been deprived of the one thing that had cemented the social structure of their race—the Flower of Life; and more importantly, they were novices in this game called warfare. On the other hand, the Masters were adepts, addicted to Protoculture, obsessed with control, and driven to transform themselves—not through any measure of spiritual evolution, but through sheer conquest of the material realm. Profligate, they lived for excess; cloned a race of warrior giants to police their empire, then, still not content, cloned an entire society they could rule at whim. They took the best specimens with them when they abandoned Tirol; all that remained were the three Elders of their race, several hundred imperfect clones—lost without their clonemasters—and Tirol's preclone population of humanoids, who were of no use to the ascended Masters.

Tirol, the third of Fantoma's twelve moons, was not the Masters' original homeworld; but they had successfully transplanted themselves on that utterly barren planetoid from one of the outer satellites. Tiresia, the capital, a blend of Tirol's analogue of Greco-Roman architecture and ultra-tech design, was the only occupied city; and as such was aware of the Invid's coming ahead of time.

Aware . . . but hardly prepared.

Early-warning sirens and howlers had the humanoid population scurrying for shelters beneath the city well in advance of the midnight attack. The clones wandered the streets in a kind of daze, while the Elders who were responsible for their reaction made certain to hide themselves away in specially-designed chambers the Masters had seen fit to construct before their mass exodus. But there were two who remained at their work while the alert sounded through the city: the scientist Cabell, and his young assistant, Rem.

"Whoever they are," Cabell was saying, while his fingers rushed a series of commands into one of the lab's data networks, "they've put down near the outpost at Rylac."

"Is their identity any doubt, Cabell?" Rem asked from behind the old man's chair. Video monitors showed a dozen burnt-orange oysterlike troop carriers hovering over a jagged ridgeline of mountains west of the city. The network spit out a data card, which Cabell immediately transferred to an adjacent on-line device.

"I don't suppose there is, my boy," the scientist said without turning around. Several of the ships had put down now, and were disgorging mecha from their forward ramps.

"Will the city's defenses save us?"

Cabell left the question unanswered; instead, he turned his attention to activation switches for the remote cameras positioned at the outpost's perimeter, his long snow-white beard grazing the control studs while he reached across the console. He was every bit a wizard of a man, portly under his tasseled robes and laurel-collared capes, with a hairless knobbed skull and thick white eyebrows, mustache, and beard. He was indeed old enough to be the young man's father, although that wasn't precisely the case. Rem was tall and slender, with an ageless, almost elfin face and a thick shock of slate-blue hair. He wore a tight-fitting uniform with a long cape of royal blue.

"We're defenseless," Rem said a moment later, reacting to Cabell's silence. "Only the old and the sick remain on Tirol."

"Quiet!" the scientist told him. The central viewscreen showed the transports lifting off. Energy-flux schematics scrolled across half-a-dozen lesser screens. "Now what could they have in mind?"

Rem gestured to a secondary video monitor. "Frankly, Cabell, I'm more concerned about these monsters they've left behind." Waves of armored, felinelike creatures could be seen advancing up and out of the drop zone.

Cabell leaned back from the console to contemplate the images, right hand stroking his beard. "They resemble drones, not monsters." One of the creatures had stopped in its tracks and seemed to be staring at the camera. Cabell brought the lens to bear on the thing, focusing in on the four-legged creature's razor-sharp claws, fangs, and shoulder horns.

"It spotted the remote!" Rem said, as the cat's eyes began to glow. An instant later a metal-shod claw swiped at the camera; the image de-rezzed, and the screen crackled with static.

The Invid were a long way from home—if Optera could still be thought of in those terms. That their strikes against the Masters' empire were fueled by revenge was true enough; but the conquest of worlds like Karbarra, Praxis, and Spheris had had a more consequential purpose, for all these planets had been seeded by Zor with the Flowers of Life—the renegade scientist's final attempt at recompense for the horrors his discoveries had inadvertently unleashed. But the resultant Flowers had proved a sterile crop, mutated at best; and so the search was under way for the one key that could unlock the mysteries of Zor's science: the Protoculture matrix he himself had hidden aboard the Superdimensional Fortress.

The legendary device had never been uncovered by Lang's teams of Robotechnicians, and now that ship lay buried under tons of earth, rock, and Macross debris far from where the Invid were directing their quest. But at the time they had no way of knowing these things.

The Flowers had been their primary concern—their nutrient grail—but that purpose had undergone a slight perversion since Zor's death at the hands of Invid troopers. For not only had he transgressed by seducing the Flowers' secret from the Invid Regis; he had also spread a kind of contagion among that race—a pathology of emulation. And within a generation the Invid had refashioned themselves, and, with a form of self-generated Protoculture, created their own galactic war machine—a fleet of disc-shaped starships, a strike force of bipedal crablike mecha, and an army of mindless battle drones—the so-called Inorganics. But this was chiefly the work of the Invid Regent, not their Queen, and a schism had resulted—one that would ultimately affect Earth's fragile hold on its future.

The Invid fleet was anchored in space above Tirol when word spread through the ranks that the Regent himself had decided to take charge of the invasion. Companies of Inorganics had already been deployed on the moon's surface to counter ground-force resistance. Now, aboard the fleet flagship, one thousand Invid troops stood at attention in the docking bay, backed by more than two hundred Pincer assault mecha.

The unarmored individual Invid was primate in shape. Bilaterally symmetrical, they stood anywhere from six to eight feet tall, and walked upright on two powerfully-muscled legs. Equally massive were the forearms, shoulders, and three-fingered hands, with their opposable thumbs. The bulbous head and huge neck—often held parallel to the ground—approximated that of a snail, with an eye on either side, and two sensory antennae at the snout. The skin was green, almost reptilian, and there was at this stage no sexual differentiation. The Regent himself was by and large a grander, nearly twenty-foot-high version of the same design, save for his purple hue and the organic cowl that rested upon his back like some sort of manta ray. This hood, which could puff like a cobra's at times, was ridged front to back with tubercle-like sensors that resembled eyeballs.

The commander of flagship troops genuflected as the hatchway to the Regent's ship hissed up, spilling brilliant light against the soldier's crimson body armor. Helmet snout lowered to the floor, the trooper brought its right hand to its breast in salute.

"My lord, the Inorganics have met only token resistance on Tirol," the commander reported, its voice distorted by the helmet filters. "So far there is no sign of the Robotech Masters."

The Regent remained on the shuttle's rampway, his bulk and flowing blue robe filling the hatch.

"Cowering beneath their beds, no doubt," the Regent said in a voice so deep it seemed to emanate from the ship itself.

The commander raised its head some, with a whirring of mechanical adjusters. "Our beloved Regis has expressed some displeasure with your strategy, my lord." It offered up a cassettelike device in its left hand. "She wanted this to be given to you."

"A voice imprint?" the Regent said dubiously. "How thoughtful of my *wife*." He snatched the cassette in his hand. "I can hardly wait to hear it."

He activated the device as he moved from the docking bay into one of the flagship's corridors. The commander and a ten-trooper squad marched in formation behind him, their armored footfalls echoing in the massive space.

"Do you truly believe that you'll find what you seek on this wretched planet?" the synthesized female voice began. *"If so you are even a greater fool than I ever suspected. This idiotic invasion of yours is the most—"*

"I've heard about enough of that," the Regent said, deactivating the voice. "Tell me, where is our *beloved* Regis?" he asked the commander after a moment.

"She has returned to her fleet flagship, my lord." When the Regent had reached his quarters, the commander thought to ask, "Shall I tell her you wish to see her, my lord?"

"Negative," the Regent said sternly. "The farther she is, the better I like it. See to it that my pets are brought aboard, and let the invasion proceed without her."

The Invid squad snapped to as the door hissed closed.

The humanoid soldiers at the Rylac outpost were easily overrun. Given the few weapons at their disposal, they made a valiant stand, but the Inorganics proved too much for them. The forward assault wave was comprised solely of Invid feline mecha; but behind these Hellcats marched companies of Scrim and Crann and Odeon—Invid robot analogues, which in some ways resembled skeletal versions of their own Shock Troopers and Pincer Ships, a demonic, bipedal infantry.

A schematic representation of a Scrim came to life on one of Cabell's monitor screens, rotating and shifting through a series of perspectives, as intact remotes from the Rylac sector continued to bring the action home to the lab.

"There is only one species capable of producing such a device," Cabell commented flatly.

"The Invid," said Rem. "It was only a matter of time."

"The strategy is typical of them: they won't descend until their fighting drones have cleared away the resistance. And after they've devastated Tirol, they'll leave these things behind to police us." Hellcat schematics were taking shape on the monitors. "These machines are puzzling, though. It's almost as if . . ."

Rem looked back and forth between the screens and the old man's face, trying to discern Cabell's meaning. "It's hopeless, isn't it?"

"I'm not saying that, my boy," the scientist replied, leaning in to study the data flows. "This feline drone is like its two-legged counterparts: computer-driven and incapable of independent action. Its functions, therefore, must be controlled by an external centralized power source of some kind." He swiveled around in his chair to gaze at his assistant. "That is its weakness, the one flaw in the system, and we must take advantage of it."

"Cabell—"

"Is it not easier to attack one target than a thousand? If we can locate that power source and disable it, then all these dreaded machines will be deactivated."

Alert lamps flashed in another part of the room and Cabell swung around to them. "The Inorganics are closing on the city. Now we'll see how they fare against real firepower."

"The Bioroids!" Rem said excitedly.

"They're our only hope."

Rick and Max had shuttled down to the surface simply to ride back up with Lisa, Miriya, Lang, and other members of the mission command team. Both men were aware that the short trip constituted their last visit to Earth for an indeterminate period of time, but neither of them made much of this. Max was still nursing some concerns about leaving Dana behind, but was otherwise fully committed to the mission. Rick, on the other hand, was so preoccupied with the wedding that he had begun to think of the mission as a simpler and more certain voyage. So it was during the return trip that he was paying almost no attention to the discussion taking place in the command shuttle conference chambers.

"I only hope this plan works," Jonathan Wolff was saying. "Coming in disguised as a Zentraedi ship . . . It could backfire on us."

"Oh, you're forgetting your own Earth history, Colonel," the Zentraedi ambassador told him. "The Greeks and their Trojan horse."

"I think you're confusing history and mythology, Lord Exedore. Wouldn't you agree, Admiral? Admiral?" Wolff repeated.

Rick surfaced from his own thoughts to find everyone at the table staring at him. "Huh? Sorry, I was, um, thinking about something else."

Wolff recapped the exchange: justification for the disguise had been something of an issue from the start. Exedore and Lang were of the opinion that Tirol's defenses would annihilate any ship that registered an alien signature. According to the Zentraedis, the Robotech Masters had been at war for generations with a race called the Invid, and any unannounced entry into the Valivarre system would be tantamount to an act of aggression. Wolff, however, along with several other members of the general staff, advanced the view that the Zentraedi themselves might no longer be considered welcome guests. After all, they had not only failed in their mission to reclaim the SDF-1, but had allied themselves with the very "Micronians" their armada had been ordered to destroy.

Wolff was a persuasive speaker, and while Rick listened he couldn't help but be impressed by the scope of the man's learning. Handsome, articulate, an inspired commander and deadly hand-to-hand combatant, the full bird colonel was considered something of a glamour boy; he favored wraparound sunglasses, wore his dark hair slicked back, and his mustache well-trimmed. But the leader of the notorious "Wolff Pack" was anything but glamorous in the field. Wolff had made a name for himself and his Hover-tank ground unit during the Southland's Malcontent Uprisings, where he had first come to the attention of Max Sterling. When the Zentraedis who survived those days spoke of Wolff, one couldn't help but hear the mixture of reverence and dread in their voices; and anyone who had read the declassified documents covering the Control Zone mop-up ops had no trouble understanding why Wolff and Breetai were often mentioned in the same breath.

"I'm just saying that disguising the ship and loading it down with mecha only serves to undermine the so-called diplomatic thrust of the mission." Wolff snorted. "No wonder Leonard and the Southern Cross brass tried to make mincemeat out of you down there."

"What do they expect us to do?" Max wanted to know. "Go in there flying a white flag? At least we've got some bargaining power this way."

"Let's just hope we won't need to use any of it," Rick said at last, straining against his seat harness. "Without the Zentraedi, the Masters could be defenseless for all we know."

Exedore shook his head. "Oh, I wouldn't count on that, Admiral." Breetai had already briefed everyone on the mecha the Masters had been developing before Zor's death —Hoverships and Bioroids.

"Gentlemen, the time is long past for arguments about strategy," Lang cut in before Rick could speak. "We've all supported this plan, and it seems rather late in the day to be changing our mind."

"I agree," Max said.

"Look, *I* agree," Wolff wanted the table to know. "I'd just like us to agree on an approach. Are we going in with fists raised or hands up? The Masters aren't going to be fooled by our outward appearance—not for long, at any rate."

"Possibly not," Exedore answered him. "But if we allow *possibilities* to influence us, we'll never leave orbit."

"I've got as many doubts as anybody," Rick said from the head of the table. "But the time's come to put them behind us. We've made our bed, as the saying goes . . ."

Brave Talk, Hunter, he thought, listening to his own words. *And I'll keep telling myself that when I'm walking down the aisle.*

Two RDF officers were watching the approach of the command shuttle from a rectangular bay in one of the factory satellite's peripheral pods. One was a slim and eager-eyed young major who had recently been appointed adjutant to General T. R. Edwards; and the other was the general himself, his disfiguration concealed beneath an irregularly-shaped black-alloy plate that covered most of the right side of his face and more than half his skull. On the uncovered left side of his head, long blond hair fell in waves to the collar of his tight-fitting uniform. He was high-cheekboned and square-jawed, and might have been considered handsome even with the plate, were it not for the cruelty in his eye and downward-turning mouth.

"So tell me, Benson," Edwards said, while his one eye continued to track the shuttle's course, "what do you know about the illustrious vice admiral?"

"I know that Hunter's one of our most decorated heroes, sir," Benson reported to the general's broad back. "Leader of the Skull during the Robotech War, commander of the RDF after the destruction of the superdimensional fortresses, about to marry the admiral . . . That's about it, sir."

Edwards clasped his hands behind his back. "That's

right. The high command likes to award medals to people who end up in the right place at the right time."

"Sir?" Benson asked.

"Anything in your academy history books about Roy Fokker?" Edwards said nastily over his shoulder. "Now there was a real VT ace for you. I remember turning those blue skies red trying to nail his ass . . . But you're too young to remember the Global War, aren't you, Benson? The real heroes." Edwards leaned forward and pressed his fingertips against the bay's permaplas viewport. "Fokker taught Hunter everything he knew, did you know that? You might even say that Hunter is what Fokker would've been, Major—that Hunter *is* Fokker."

Benson swallowed hard, unsure how to respond, uncertain if he even should.

Edwards touched his skullplate, remembering, forcing himself back over tormented terrain—to what was left of Alaska Base after Zentraedi annihilation bolts had destroyed the Grand Cannon and made a hell of that icebound site. And how one man and one woman had survived. The woman was unharmed, protected where she cowered while her father had fried alive; but the man, *how he had suffered*! What agony he had endured, down on his knees shamelessly trying to push the ruins of an eye back where it belonged, fingers pinched in an effort to knit together flesh that had been opened on his face and forehead. Then the rapture he had known when a solitary Veritech had appeared out of those unnatural clouds. But it was the *woman* that VT pilot had come for, and no other. It was the *woman* who had been flown to safety, the *woman* who had risen through the ranks, while the man had been left behind to die, to rot in that alien-made inferno . . .

"Ah, what a wedding this will be, Benson," Edwards continued after a moment of angry silence. "Admirals Rick

Hunter and Lisa Hayes. Star-crossed lovers, if ever there were. Born and reborn for each other."

"Till death do them part," Benson returned with a uncomfortable laugh.

Edwards spun on his heels, face contorted, then erupting in laughter. "Yes, Major, *how right you are!*"

Most of the Zentraedi had been off scouring the galaxy for Zor's ship and its hidden Protoculture matrix when the Robotech Masters first perfected the Bioroids. Sixty-foot-tall nontransformable goliath knights piloted by low-level clones, they were meant to act as the Masters' police force on the remote worlds that comprised Tirol's empire, freeing the Zentraedi for further acts of conquest and continued warfare against the Invid. The Masters had never considered that Protoculture would one day be in limited supply, nor that their army of giant warriors would be defeated in a distant corner of the Fourth Quadrant by so simple a weapon as love. So it fell on the Bioroids by chance and Protoculture's own dark designs, to defend the Masters' empire against Optera's ravenous horde. But try as they might, they were no match for the Invid Shock Troopers and Pincer Ships, with their plasma weapons and energy discs. And as Protoculture grew more and more scarce, they could barely defend against the mindless Inorganics.

"It is sheer numbers," Cabell explained to Rem as they watched Tiresia's first line of defense fall. The clonemasters left behind to rule the Bioroid pilots were an inferior lot, so the fight was not all it should have been. *The Masters have thrown them our world*, Cabell left unsaid. Those massive spade fortresses with their clone populations were the Masters' new homes; they had no plans to return to Tirol.

Command-detonated mines took out wave after wave of

Hellcats, but this did little more than delay the inevitable. The Bioroids dug in, finding cover behind hastily-erected barricades, and fired until their cannons and assault rifles went red-hot and depleted. And when the Inorganics began to overrun their lines, they went hand-to-claw with the marauders, employing last-stand tactics worthy of history's finest. Cabell could feel no sympathy for them as such; but staring at the lab's central viewscreen he was overcome by a greater sense of pathos and loss. External mikes picked up the clones' anguished cries, their desperate utterances to one another in that raspy, almost synthesized voice the Masters so loved.

"There's too many of them!" the pilot of a blue Bioroid told his teammates along the front, before two Hellcats leaped and crashed through the mecha's visorlike face-shield. A second blue blasted the intruders with the last of his weapon's charge, only to fall an instant later, Inorganics ripping at the machine's armor in a mad effort to get to the pilot within.

Disgusted, Cabell stood up and reached across the console to shut down the audio transmissions. "The Flower of Life, that's what they've come for," he told his apprentice in a tired voice.

"But that plant hasn't been present in this sector for generations," Rem said, slipping into the padded con chair.

"Then they'll want the matrix. Or failing that, vengeance for what the Masters ordered done to their world."

Rem turned his attention to the screen. Scrim devils and Hellcats were tearing through the Bioroid base, eyes aglow like hot coals, fangs slick with the clone pilots' blood. "They'll rip the planet apart looking for something they'll never find."

"No one ever accused the Invid of being logical, my boy, only thorough."

"Then the city will fall next. Those drones are unstoppable."

"Nonsense," Cabell exclaimed, anger in his voice. "They may be intimidating, but they're not unstoppable."

Rem shot to his feet. "Then let's find their weak spot, Cabell." He drew a handgun from beneath his cape and armed it. "And for that, we're going to require a specimen."

CHAPTER
THREE

> Try as he might to offset the suffering his discoveries had un-
> leashed, Zor's mistakes kept piling up, compounding themselves.
> He'd sent his ship to Earth only to have the Zentraedi follow it
> there; he'd hidden the matrix so well that the Masters had ample
> time to wage their war; his seeded worlds had drawn the Invid
> ... What remained but the final injustice?—that by trying to repli-
> cate his very form and drives, the Regent and Regis should
> become prisoners of appetites they had never before experienced.
> Is it any mystery why even the Masters banished his image
> throughout their empire?

> Bloom Nesterfig, *The Social Organization of the Invid*

BRIGADIER GENERAL REINHARDT, HAVING SHUTTLED
up to the factory earlier that day, was on hand to meet the
mission command team. He informed Lang, Lord Exedore,
Lisa, and Rick that things were still running on schedule;
the last shiploads of supplies and stores were on their way
up from Earth even now, and most of the 10,000 who
would make up the crew were already aboard the satellite,
many aboard the SDF-3 itself. Max and Miriya joined the
others by an enormous hexagonal viewport that overlooked
the null-gee central construction hold. They were joined
after a moment by Colonel Wolff and Jean Grant, who had
Bowie and Dana by the hand.

The view from here was fore to aft along the underside

of the fortress. Lisa often wished that the bow wasn't quite so, well, *phallic*—the euphemism she employed in mixed company. But the twin booms of the main gun were just that: like two horned, tumescent appendages that took up nearly a third of the crimson ship's length. If the weapon had none of the awesome firepower of the SDF-1's main gun, at least it had the *look* of power to it. Autowelders and supply shuttles were moving through the hold's captured sunlight, and a crew of full-size Zentraedi were at work on one of the sky-blue sensor blisters along the fortress's port side.

"How many kilometers out will we have to be before we can fold?" Wolff wanted to know. Everyone remembered all too plainly what had happened when the SDF-1 attempted to fold while still in the vicinity of Macross Island.

"Lunar orbit will suffice," Exedore told him. "Doctor Lang and Breetai concur on this."

"Speak of the devil," Lisa said, looking around the hold, "I thought he was supposed to meet us here."

Miriya laughed shortly. "He probably forgot."

"He's been pretty busy," Rick offered.

"Well, we can't wait," Reinhardt said, running a hand over his smooth pate. "We've got a lot of last-minute details to attend to and—"

Everyone reacted to Dana's gasp at the same moment, turning first to the child's startled face, then to the hatchway she had her eyes fixed on.

There was a giant standing here.

Half the gathered group knew him as a sixty-footer, of course, but even micronized Breetai was an impressive sight: almost eight feet of power dressed in a uniform more befitting a comic book hero than a Zentraedi commander, and wearing a masklike helmet that left only his mouth and lantern jaw exposed.

Before anyone could speak, he had moved in and one-hand heaved Lisa and Miriya atop each of his shoulders. His voice boomed. "So I'm not important enough to wait for, huh? You Micronians are an impatient lot."

He let the women protest a moment before setting them back down on the floor.

"I never thought I'd see you like this again," Lisa said, tugging her uniform back into shape. The only other time Breetai had permitted himself to undergo the reduction process was during the search of the SDF-1 for the Protoculture matrix.

"It takes a man to give away a bride," Breetai said in all seriousness, "not a giant."

Dawn marked Tiresia's doom. The troop carriers returned, yawning catastrophe; but this time it wasn't Inorganics they set loose, but the crablike Shock Troopers and Pincer Ships. They attacked without mercy, skimming discs of white annihilation into the streets, dwellings, and abandoned temples. The humanoid populace huddled together in shelters, while those masterless clones who had become the city's walking dead surrendered and burned. Left to fend for themselves, the old and infirm tried to hide from the invaders, but it was hardly a day to play games with the Reaper: his minions were everywhere, and within hours the city was laid to waste.

Cannon muzzles and missile racks sprang from hidden emplacements, spewing return fire into the void, and once again the Bioroids faced the storm and met their end in heroic bursts of orange flame and blinding light. From the depths of the pyramidal Royal Hall rode an elite unit on saucer-shaped Hovercraft outfitted with powerful disc guns and particle-beam weapons systems. They joined the Invid in an airborne dance of devastation, coupling obscenely in the city skies, exchanging thundering volleys of quantum death.

Morning was filled with the corkscrewing trails of angry projectiles and crisscrossed with hyphens and pulses of colored light. Spherical explosions strobed overhead, rivaling the brightness of Fantoma's own primary, low in the east behind clouds of debris. Mecha fell like a storm of blazing hail, cutting fiery swaths across the cityscape.

Here a Pincer Ship put down to give chase to an old man its discs had thrown clear from a Hoverchair. Frustrated, the Invid trained its weapons on Tiresia's architectural wonders and commenced a deadly pirouette. Statues and ornaments slagged in the heat, and five of the antigrav columns that marked the Royal Hall's sacred perimeter were toppled.

Ultimately the Invid's blue command ships moved in, forming an unbreachable line as they marched through the city, their top-mounted cannons ablaze. Inside the shelters the citizens of Tiresia cowered and clung to one another as the footfalls of the giants' war strides shook Tirol's ravaged surface, echoing in the superheated subterranean confinement.

Cabell and Rem had chosen a deserted, now devastated sector for their Hellcat hunt. With most of Tiresia's defenses in ruin, the fierce fighting that typified the early hours of the invasion had subsided to distant hollow blasts from the few remaining contested areas. A patrol of bipedal Inorganics moved past the alley where the scientist and his assistant waited. Rem raised the muzzle of the assault rifle he had slung over one shoulder, but Cabell waved him back.

"But it doesn't sense our presence," Rem insisted, peering over Cabell's shoulder. "Now's our chance."

"No," Cabell said firmly. "I want one of the feline droids."

They began to move into the street after the Inorganic had passed. Cabell kept them to the shadows at first, then grew more brazen. Rem understood that the old man was trying to lure one of the creatures out but he had some misgivings about Cabell's method.

"I hope we snare one of them and not the other way around," he said wearily, swinging the rifle in a gentle arc.

Cabell stopped short in the center of the street as a kind of mechanical growl reached them from somewhere nearby. "I have the distinct impression our progress is being observed."

"I was about to say the same thing."

"Perhaps our behavior is puzzling to them," Cabell mused, back in motion now. "They probably expect us to run in terror."

"And I forget, why *aren't* we?" Rem started to say when another growl sounded. "Guess they're not puzzled anymore . . . Show yourself, fiend," he growled back, arming the rifle.

"There!" Cabell said all at once.

The Hellcat was glaring down at them from a low roof not twenty yards up the street, midday light caught in the beast's shoulder horns, fangs, and razor-sharp tail. Then it pounced.

"On stun!" Cabell cried, and Rem fired.

The short burst glanced off the cat's torso, confusing it momentarily, but not long enough to make a difference. It leaped straight for the two men before Rem could loose a second shot, but he did manage to shove Cabell clear of the Inorganic's path. The cat turned sharply as it landed; Rem hit it twice more to no avail.

"Get away from it, boy!" Rem heard Cabell shout. He

looked around, amazed that the old man had covered so much ground in so little time—although the Inorganic was certainly incentive enough: it was hot on Cabell's trail.

Rem chased the two of them, firing wildly, and rounded a corner in time to see his mentor barrel-ass down a rubble slide and throw himself into the cockpit of an overturned Bioroid transport ship. Fixed on its prey, the Hellcat seemed unaware of Rem, and was busy trying to claw through the ship's bubble shield. Rem reached down to up the rifle's charge, only to find the thing depleted. He was busy cursing himself when he spied a fallen Invid command ship nearby, one of its cannontips still aglow with priming charge.

Cautiously, he approached the ship, the useless weapon raised. The command plastron was partially ajar, a four-fingered hand lodged in the opening. Rem clambered up and over one of the mecha's arms and gave the hatch a violent tug, forcing the rifle down into the invader's face as he did so. But the Invid was already dead, its bulbous head and stalklike neck split wide open. Rem ignored the stench and took a quick look at the cockpit's bewildering gadgetry. The alien's right hand was hooked around what Rem decided was the trigger mechanism, and from the looks of things the Hellcat was almost perfectly centered in the cannon's reticle. Rem grunted a kind of desperate curse, slid down into the cockpit—his legs going knee-deep into a viscous green bath of nutrient fluid—and hit the trigger.

A pulsed beam of crimson light threw the Hellcat clear from the transport and left it on its side thirty feet from the transport, stunned and enveloped by a kind of St. Elmo's fire. Cabell threw open the canopy and glanced back at the crippled command ship with a bewildered expression.

"Why did you save me?" the old man yelled in Zentraedi, *lingua franca* of the Masters' empire.

Rem heard the call and was tempted to stay put for a moment, but thought better of it. He showed himself and said, "Hello, Cabell. All safe and sound? You didn't really think I'd abandon you, did you?"

The scientist scowled. "You could have killed me, you young—" He bit off his own words and laughed, resignedly. "My boy, you amaze me."

Rem jumped to the ground and approached the transport. "Frankly, I amaze myself." He looked away from the alien ship he had fired, and gestured to the Hellcat. "Now all we've got to do is figure out how to get this thing back to the lab."

"My lord, we've found no trace of the Flower of Life anywhere," the voice of an Invid lieutenant reported to the Regent.

"But that's impossible, you *idiot*!" the Regent shouted at his monitor. "This is their homeworld. They must be here! Scan the entire planet."

The flagship throne room, like the Invid castle and hives on Optera, was an organic chamber, so given over to the urgings of Protoculture that its very bulkheads and sensor devices resembled living systems of neural-tissue circuitry. Visceral greens and purples, they pulsed to rhythms dictated deep within the ship's animate drives. So, too, the contoured control couch itself, with its graceful curves, the slender arcing neck of its overhead sensor lamp, its proboscislike forward communicator tube. The Regent did not so much sit as reshape his being to the seat's demands.

On either side of him sat a Hellcat larger and more polished than any of the standard versions, with collars encrusted with gems handpicked from the spoils of a score of conquered worlds. Elsewhere, in cages, were living samples from those same worlds: sentient prisoners from Karbarra, Spheris, and the rest.

"We have searched, my lord," the trooper continued. "The Sensor Nebula registers no presence of the Flowers. None whatsoever."

"Fools!" muttered the Regent, canceling the transmission. He could hear his wife's laughter behind him.

"Congratulations, husband," the Regis mocked him from across the room. "Once again you have impressed us all with your supreme stupidity."

"I don't like your tone," the Regent said, turning to her.

One might have almost mistaken her for a humanoid life-form; certainly she was more that than the ursoid and vulpine beings that populated the Regent's personal zoo. But at the same time there was something ethereal and insubstantial about her, an inhumanness that lurked in the depths of her cobalt eyes. Twenty feet tall and slender, she clothed her completely hairless form in a red full-length robe and curious, five-fingered tasseled gloves. Four emerald-green sensor scarabs that might have been facelike adornments decorated the robe's bracelike collar and neck closure.

"I told you the Robotech Masters were too clever to hide the matrix in their own back yard."

"Silence, *woman*!" the Regent demanded, rising from the throne.

But the Regis stood her ground. "If you hadn't been so desperate to prove yourself a great warrior, we might have sent spies to learn where they've taken it."

The Regent looked at his wife in disbelief. "Are you forgetting who got us into this predicament in the first place? *I'm* not the one who fell under the spell of Zor and allowed him to steal our Flower of Life."

"Must you keep *harping* on that!" the Regis screamed,

shutting her eyes and waving her fists in the air. "It happened a long time ago. And since then *I* have evolved, while you've remained the spoiled child you always were. You took his life; now you won't rest content until you've conquered his empire." She gestured offhandedly to the Regent's "pets" and caged life-forms. "You and your dreams of empire . . . Mark my words, husband, some day these beings will rise up to strike you down."

The Regent laughed. "Yes, you've *evolved*—into a pathetic imitation of the females of Zor's race."

"Perhaps so," she countered, arms akimbo. "But that's preferable to imitating the Masters' toys and bloodlust." She turned on her heel and headed for the door. "I'm returning to Optera."

"Stop! I forbid you to go!" the Regent told her, furious.

"Don't provoke me," she shouted from the doorway, "you spineless anachronism!"

"Wait!" the Regent demanded, cursing her. He whirled around as the door hissed closed, Tirol huge in the room's starboard viewports. "I'll show you," he muttered under his breath. "Tirol will feel my potency . . . and I'll win back your love."

"Toys," Dr. Harry Penn told Lang, an undisguised note of disapproval in his voice. "War toys, when we could be fashioning wonders." He was a large man with a gruff-looking exterior that masked the gentlest of spirits. The thick mustache and beard he had grown to mask the pock-marked, hooked-nose cragginess of his face had only ended up adding to the effect he had hoped to minimize. It was a scholarly, academic image he was after, and as the oldest member of the Plenipotentiary Council and one of Lang's top men he felt he deserved no less.

"There'll be time for that when this mission returns,"

Lang said evenly. "Until then we have to be sure of our strengths."

Penn made a disgruntled sound. "A peaceful mission, a diplomatic mission . . . Am I the only one who remembers the meaning of those words?"

The two men were standing by one of the factory's observation bays; in the blackness of space beyond, two Veritechs were being put through the paces.

These were not the first generation VTs the Skull and other teams had flown against the Zentraedi, but Alpha fighters, the latest prototypes from Lang's research department laboratories. The SDF-3's arsenal wasn't limited to these reconfigurable one-pilot craft—the last six years had seen the development of Hovertanks, Logans, and an array of new and improved Destroids—but the Veritech remained something of Robotechnology's favored child, weapon *extraordinaire* and near-symbol of the war. The Alpha VT had more armor than its older sibling; it packed almost twice the firepower and was equipped with ablative shields and detachable augmentation pods for deepspace flight. Moreover, it had the capability to link up with the so-called Beta VT—a bulkier, thin-winged variant that appeared to lack an appropriate radome—and thereby more than double its range and occupancy capabilities.

Lang indicated the blue fighter as it twisted through space, reconfiguring to Guardian, then Battloid mode. "I just wanted you to see for yourself the progress we've made, Harry."

"Sterling, here," said a voice over the ob deck's speakers. "The Alpha handled the last sequence beautifully. No sign of stress."

"Fine, Max," said Lang, directing his words to a microphone. "The prototype looks good so far. Now comes the real test," he added for Penn's benefit. "Max, Karen, move yourselves into position for trans-docking maneuver!"

Max rogered the transmission; Karen Penn, Harry's only daughter, said, "We're on our way."

Lang risked a quarter turn and found Penn regarding him with a mixture of surprise and rage. "You're awfully quiet, Harry, is something wrong?"

"Have you gone mad, Lang! You know I didn't want Karen participating in this test."

"What was I supposed to do, Harry, refuse her permission? Don't forget, she volunteered, and she's one of our most able young pilots."

"But I don't want her to get mixed up in this, Emil. Can't you understand that? *Science* is her future, not warfare."

"Control," Max's voice squawked over the speakers, "we are in position at T-niner-delta. Standing by to reconfigure and align for docking sequence."

The maneuver called for each of the Veritechs to jettison and exchange their unmanned Beta modules, blue to red, red to blue. Max carried out his part without a hitch, imaging over to fighter mode and engaging the VT's retros for a solid linkup with its sister module. But Karen slipped up. Max couldn't tell at first whether she had been too heavy-minded, or had simply misread the VT's telemetry displays. In either case she was in trouble, the blue Beta off on a ride to eternity, and Karen in what looked like a planet-bound freefall.

Max tried to reach her on the net, through a cacophony of questions and exclamations from command—most of them from Dr. Penn himself. Karen wasn't responding, but there wasn't real cause for concern—yet. Assuming she wasn't unconscious or worse—something unseen, an embolism, perhaps—Karen had ample time to get herself into the Veritech's EVA suit; and failing that, the factory could bring its tractor beam to bear. But Max wanted to see Karen pull out of this one without an assist; she was bright and full of potential, and he wanted her for the Skull.

"Stabilizers are gone," Karen said suddenly. ". . . Power surge must have fried the circuitry."

Then Dr. Penn's panicked voice bellowed in Max's ears. "Sterling, do something! You've got to help her!"

"Karen," Max said calmly. "Go to Guardian and bring your thrusters into play. I'm right behind you if they fail."

"Roger, Skull leader," Karen returned.

On the factory ob deck, Penn muscled his way through a crowd of techs to get close to the monitor screen. He sucked in his breath seeing his daughter's red Alpha in a slow-motion end-over-end fall; but the next instant found the VT reconfigured, its bird-of-prey foot thrusters burning bright in the night. And in another moment she was out of danger and there were hoots and hollers ringing in his ears, tears of release in his eyes.

Lang and Penn were waiting in the docking bay when the VTs came in. Max missed the days of flattop touch-downs, the cat officers and their impromptu launch dances; but the *Daedalus* and *Prometheus* supercarriers were part of the SDF-1 burial mound now, and unnecessary in any case.

"Karen, thank God you're all right!" Max heard Dr. Penn call out as the blue's canopy slid open. "That little escapade nearly gave me a heart attack."

Guilt's his game, Max thought as he climbed out of Skull One.

"Well, if you were scared, imagine how I felt," Karen was telling her father. "I'm still shaking."

Penn waved a forefinger at her. "This proves once and for all you've no business being a test pilot."

"Don't overdo it, Dad." Karen removed her thinking

cap, spilling honey-blond hair to her shoulders. She had small delicate features, eyes the color of pre-Columbian jade. "I'm a professional. This stuff comes with the territory."

"I'll say she is," Max chimed in before Penn could get in another word. "That linkup wasn't her fault. Dollars to donuts you'll find some glitch in the guidance computers."

Penn glared at him. "I'm sure you mean well, Commander, but all this is—"

"Meaning well has nothing to do with it. I just don't want to see Ensign Penn's talents go to waste. She impressed me, Dr. Penn—and I'm not easily impressed."

Penn blanched some; he wasn't about to debate Sterling's words. But Karen was still his daughter. "Well, I'm not impressed," he told Karen after Max had walked off. "I have others plans for you."

She flashed him a look he remembered from way back and started to move off, but Dr. Lang put out his hand to stop her.

"Karen, a moment please."

"You gonna chew me out now?"

"Calm down," said Lang. "I'm going to recommend you for assignment to a Veritech team."

"Just a minute, Emil," Penn said, one hand clasped around Karen's upper arm. "Don't you think you're overstepping your authority?" He had already lost his wife, and Karen's joining the RDF had threatened to destroy what had once been a close relationship. Now Lang seemed bent on trying to scuttle what small joy he had left.

Lang pried his friend's fingers open and motioned Karen along. "I'm sorry, Harry, but she's old enough to make up her own mind. You can't hold on to her forever.

Besides, if this mission *should* encounter resistance, we're going to need experienced pilots."

"Resistance," Penn snorted, and began to storm off. But half-a-dozen steps away he swung around. "All the more reason to hold on to her for as long as I can."

CHAPTER
FOUR

Evidence points to the existence of a plethora of mystery cults in the years immediately preceding Tirol's so-called Great Transition (i.e., that period in which most of the moon's humanoid population were put to death and the Robotech Masters began their extensive cloning experiments). In fact, some of these cults survived well into the First Period . . . The labyrinth, apparently, was constructed for ritual use, and the Pyramidal Royal Hall added later as that subterranean cult gave way to one of stellar orientation. Several commentators have felt compelled to bring Minoans, Egyptians, and the Maya into the discussions but aside from certain structural similarities, there was little in common between Tirol and Earth's religions.

History of the Second Robotech War
Volume CCXVI, "Tirol"

WITH THE WEDDING ONLY A DAY OFF NOW, RICK SAT in his soon-to-be-vacated quarters aboard the factory satellite contemplating the future. Earth hung in the blackness of the viewport behind the desk. Around him were stacked boxes of personal items he had accumulated over the course of the last four years: photographs, citations— memorabilia dating back to his late father's air circus, the SDF-1 and New Macross before the storm. He came across a snapshot taken by a robocam unit of Minmei standing by the Macross park's fountain; poking out from the top of a shopping bag were two posters of the singing star from those early days: one an RDF enlistment ad, and the second a Miss Macross pinup. On the recent side, Lisa was equally well represented. But the more Rick pored through these things the more depressed he became. He had no doubts about his love for Lisa, but what would it mean to abandon all this space and free time he had grown accustomed to? Not that there had been much of either, given mission priorities and such, but the *idea* of personal time, the options. Rick's hand was actually trembling while he packed. He had begun to wonder whether a drink might help, and was reaching for the bottle he kept around for special occasions, when Vince Grant announced himself at the door and stepped in.

At just a shade under seven feet, Grant was the only man aboard who could come close to filling Breetai's shoes. He had brown skin and close-cropped tight curls, and a long face lent a certain nobility by his broad forehead and chiseled features. His dark eyes were bright and full of expression, and he was a man known to speak his mind, consequence be damned. Technically, he was Rick's adjutant, a commander, but he was also attached to rapid deployment's new all-terrain mobile base, the Ground Military Unit, or GMU. Grant had headed up a crackerjack Excaliber unit in New Macross, but Rick hadn't really gotten to know him until after the death of his sister, Claudia.

"Just wanted to see if you needed help with anything, sir," Vince said, offering a casual salute.

Rick turned a sullen face to the assortment of bags and boxes piled about. "Not unless you're good at juggling."

"What, these?" Vince said uncertainly.

"No, Vince, the past and future."

"Sir?"

Rick waved dismissively. "Forget it. What's on your mind, Vince?"

Vince took a breath. "Edwards, sir."

"General Edwards?" Suspicion rose in Rick's eyes. "What about him?"

"Would the general have any reason for acting against our best interests, sir? I mean, is there something I'm not privy to that might explain certain . . . *proclivities*?"

"'Proclivities'?" said Rick. "Say what's on your mind."

In a rush, Vince said, "It just seems to me that the man has some designs of his own. I'm not saying that it's anything I can put my finger on, but for starters there's his friendship with Leonard and that character Zand. You've been busy, sir, and preoccupied. You're insulated from the scuttlebutt—"

"If you have allegations," Rick broke in, "you'd better be prepared to back them up with some hard facts. Now, do you have any—yes or no?"

Tight-lipped all at once, Vince shook his head. "Only hearsay, sir."

Rick mulled it over after he dismissed Vince. The idea of going halfway across the galaxy with a divided crew was hardly a comforting thought. And in fact there was an underlying feeling of disunity that continued to plague the mission. Lang and Exedore on one side, Edwards and the political machine on the other, with the Southern Cross somewhere in between . . . Rick tried to put together what he knew of Edwards. Roy Fokker had often spoken of Edwards's self-serving allegiances during the Global Civil War, his later alignment with Admiral Hayes, Lisa's father, and the Grand Cannon project; but then, that was years ago, and a lot of good men had been lured over to the UEDC's side. In the decade since, Edwards had become a force to be reckoned with in Monument City, and a respected officer in the RDF. Presently, as leader of the infamous Ghost Squadron, he had what amounted to an unassailable power base.

It was with all this on his mind that Rick went in search of Max and some objective input.

But it was Lisa he found in the Sterlings' quarters.

She was standing behind the dummied gown he wasn't meant to see until tomorrow.

"Isn't this supposed to be bad luck or something?" Rick asked, looking back and forth between Miriya and Lisa.

"Don't go getting superstitious on me, mister." Lisa laughed. "Besides, I'm not *in* the dress." She stepped out from behind the dressmaker's dummy and saluted stiffly. "Now show some respect."

Rick played along, snapping to and apologizing.

"Impending marriage is no excuse for relaxing discipline."

I'll have to remember that, Rick thought as he approached Lisa and took her by the waist. "Hi," he said softly.

"I beg your pardon, Admiral, but aren't you exceeding your authority?"

Rick pulled her close. "I can't help myself, ma'am. So take away my star, throw me in the brig. But please, not until the honeymoon's over . . ."

Miriya made a sour face and turned to Max, who had entered unobserved. "Sounds more like a court-martial than a marriage."

Max allowed the lovers a brief kiss before announcing himself, and five minutes later he and Rick were on their way to the factory's combat-simulation staging area, where Max had a young ensign he wanted Rick to meet. En route they discussed Edwards, but Max didn't have much to offer in the way of facts or advice. Lang was the one Rick needed to speak with, Sterling suggested, and until then the less said the better.

Cadets underwent actual mecha and weapons training in

the factory's null-gee core, and out on Moon Base; but it was during sim-time that a cadet faced combat scenarios, and psychological profiles were established and evaluated. Robotechnicians took a good deal of pride in what they had created in the staging area, with projecbeam and holographic effects of such intensity that even veterans were sometimes overwhelmed. The object was not, however, to score bull's-eyes or dazzle the audience with space combat maneuvers, but to demonstrate that one could keep cool under fire and make prudent, often split-second decisions.

Jack Baker was the ensign Max had in mind. Rick watched him being run through one of the advanced scenarios, designed to place the trainee in a position where he or she would have to decide between adherence to command dictates or altruistic heroics. Rick had little fondness for the scenario, because it happened to feature him—a holo-likeness of Rick, at any rate—as the downed pilot, awash in a 3-D sea. For want of an actual enemy, cadets found themselves up against stylized ersatz Zentraedi Battlepods.

Baker's scores were well above average throughout the first portion of the scenario, but ultimately they dropped to standard after the ensign opted to go after his downed wingman, instead of following orders to reengage.

"Not the smoothest performance," Max commented, "but you have to admit he's got something."

"Yeah," Rick nodded. "But I'm not sure it's something I like."

Baker was ordered up to the control booth, and joined Rick and Max there a few minutes later. He was a slight but energetic youth, with thick, unruly carrot-colored hair and bushy eyebrows. Blue-eyed, pale, and freckled, he impressed Rick as something of a discipline problem. At the same time, though, Baker was forceful and determined; a seat-of-the-pants pilot, a natural.

"Sir, I know my performance wasn't perfect," Baker started right in. "But that test wasn't a fair demonstration of my abilities."

Rick wagged a gloved finger in the ensign's face. "In the first place, you went off auto-pilot, contrary to orders. Second, by doing so you endangered the rest of the team. And *third*, you didn't even manage to *rescue* me."

"Yes, but—"

"Dismissed, Ensign."

"But, sir, I—"

"You heard the admiral," Max chimed in.

Baker closed his mouth and saluted. "I appreciate the admiral's input, sir," he managed before he left.

"Funny, but he reminds me of someone," Max said, watching Baker walk away. "Flyboy by the name of Hunter, if memory serves."

"I guess he does have a certain reckless sense of style about him."

"And I suppose that's why you were so hard on him, huh?"

"Just trying to improve him as a team player, Max. Besides," Rick added with a laugh, "the look on his face was priceless."

Max accompanied Rick back to his quarters after they had watched a few more cadets and officers run through the simulator. Rick was in a reminiscent mood, so they talked about the first time they had set foot in the factory after *liberating* it from Commander Reno, and about baby Dana's part in that op. Max wanted to talk about leaving

Dana behind now, but Rick didn't seem to want to surrender his train of thought.

The factory was buzzing with activity; shuttles were arriving every few hours with supplies and personnel, and boarding of the SDF-3 was under way, with techs lined up for last minute briefings, assignments, and med-scans from Jean Grant's extensive med staff. In another area of the satellite, maintenance crews, carpenters, and caterers were setting up for the wedding.

"And it's not just the wedding," Rick was saying when they entered his quarters. "I keep thinking about the enormity and importance of this mission. Maybe . . . maybe we've taken on too much this time."

"I hope you're not going to start in about how you're the youngest admiral in the force, and how undeserving you are."

"The best and the brightest," Rick said to his reflection in the viewport. "That's me."

Just then the door tone sounded and T. R. Edwards strode in on Rick's welcome.

"Hope I'm not disturbing you, Admiral."

"What's on your mind, General?"

"Why, I just wanted to wish you good luck, Hunter."

Rick noted that Edwards's faceplate made it difficult to tell whether he was sincere. And it was just as difficult for Rick to put Vince Grant's suspicions from his mind.

"What d'you mean by that, Edwards?" Rick said defensively.

Edwards showed a surprised look and turned an uncertain glance to Max. "Well, the wedding, of course. What else would I mean?"

"Oh, oh of course," Rick said, getting to his feet. He extended his hand. "Thanks, Edwards."

"Admiral Hayes's daughter," Edwards mused while they shook hands. "Imagine that . . . The irony of it, I mean. No love lost between you and him back then, was there?"

Rick stared into Edwards's eye.

"Oh, I'm sorry, Admiral. I guess you don't like to remember those days." Edwards relaxed his grip and walked to the door. "Just wanted to say good luck. To you, too, Sterling."

Rick and Max exchanged baffled looks as the door hissed shut.

Cabell and Rem had managed to get the Hellcat back to the lab undetected; it was no easy task, but a little muscle power and an abandoned Hovercar did the trick. Cabell had the Inorganic on one of the scanner tables now. He had rendered it harmless by removing a transponder from the machine's flank. Having witnessed Bioroids blowing Hellcats to bits—literally—it came as no surprise to find that the thing was hollow, its entire circuitry contained in its thick skin. But if Cabell had discovered *how* it worked, the source of its power remained a mystery—one he hoped to solve by analyzing the transponder.

On the other side of the room, Rem was up to his ears in Pollinators. Explosions had loosed them from their cage and they were all over him, now, screeching up a storm, attaching themselves to his arms, legs, and neck, and trying desperately to bury themselves in the folds of his long cloak. They might have passed for small white, mop-head dogs, except for their muffinlike paws and knob-ended horns. For a long while Zor had kept their secret from the Tirolian elite, but eventually the Masters had discovered the crucial part they played in spreading the Flower of

Life. So Zor went a step further and hid most of the creatures, naming Cabell as their guardian.

"What's happening to these things!" Rem shouted in a muffled voice, pulling one from his face. "They're going crazy!"

"They have a biogenetic link to the Flower," the old man answered calmly, hefting the Hellcat's transponder. "The presence of the Invid is disturbing to them."

"And to me," Rem started to say, when something truly monstrous appeared on one of the viewscreens. It was an enormous ship, he decided at once—because nothing so ghastly green and hideous could live in the real world. Its central head and torso resembled a kind of armored, humpbacked slug with two mandibularly-horned lizard heads on segmented necks arising Siamese-like from where arms might have been. There were three tails, two of which were tapered with stinger ends, and eight legs protruding from a suckered belly more appropriate for a sea creature than a terrestrial behemoth.

Cabell narrowed his eyes at the screen and grunted. "Their Enforcer transport. It's meant to frighten us into submission. It's captives they want now, my boy."

His thoughts turned briefly to the three Elders, who had secreted themselves somewhere in Tiresia's labyrinthine underground. *What the Invid Regent would give for their fey hides*, Cabell thought. He began to consider using them as a bargaining chip for the release of Tirol's surviving populace if it came to that, but judged it best to let that decision rest until the moment came. Safety for himself and the boy was all that concerned him just now.

"Cabell, we've got to abandon the lab," Rem said, as renewed fighting shook the city. "We can't allow your research to fall into their hands."

"I've got what I need," Cabell told him, indicating the transponder. He began to gather up data cards and chips; then, as he activated a bank of switches above the main console, two floor panels slid open, revealing a stairway that lead to the labyrinth beneath the Royal Hall. In times prior to the Great Transition, the labyrinth had been used for religious rituals.

"What about the Pollinators?"

"Take them. We'll need them if we're ever to duplicate Zor's experiments."

Rem suppressed a curse as the Pollinators he had pried from his uniform reattached themselves, screeching their mad songs all the while. He hesitated at the top of the dark staircase.

"Do we stay down here until the Invid leave?"

Cabell laughed from the blackness deeper in. "Till they leave? You're an optimist, my boy."

From his quarters on the Invid flagship, the Regent watched the descent of the Menace with obvious delight. In a moment the hydra-ship was bellowing its arrival, three sets of jaws opening to belch forth squadrons of Enforcer troops, the invasion group's mop-up crew and police force. They rode one-pilot strike ships, golden-colored tubular-shaped crafts with hooded, open-air cockpits and globular propulsion systems. They picked up where the command ships left off, dispatching what remained of Tiresia's pitiful defenses. As scenes of death and destruction played across the viewscreen, the Regent urged his troops on, mouth approximating a smile, sensor antennae suffused with color. But follow-up transmissions from the moon's surface were enough to erase that momentary blush.

"Scanners continue to register negative on all fronts, my lord."

The ground troops had completed their sweep of Tiresia, but the Regent still wasn't convinced. "You're certain there's nowhere else the Robotech Masters might have concealed the Flowers?"

"Yes, my lord. We would have detected even the slightest trace."

The Regent leaned back in the control couch. "Very well," he said after a brief silence. "I wash my hands of this wretched world. Do what you will, my legions."

He had expected an immediate response, an affirmation of his command, but instead the lieutenant risked a suggestion. "Pardon me, my lord, but shouldn't we delay the extermination until they've told us everything they know?"

"Good point," the Regent replied after he had gotten over the soldier's audacity. "Have your units round up any survivors at once, and prepare them for questioning. We shall see if we can't persuade them to tell us where their Masters have taken the Flowers of Life. I shall conduct the inquisition myself. Inform me when you have secured the city."

"It is done, my lord." The soldier signed off.

The city's temples became prisons. Those Tiresians who survived the enforcers' roundup, who survived the plasma hell they poured into the breached shelters, were packed shoulder to shoulder in improvised holding zones. They were a sorry lot, these bruised and battered sackcloth-clad humanoids; but even greater indignities awaited them. Some knew this and envied the clones, all dead now. For the first time in generations no clones walked Fantoma's moon. Save one, that is . . .

"Are they bringing more in?" a man asked his fellow

prisoners as the temple's massive door was opened, admitting light into their midst. "These monsters mean to smother us alive."

"Quiet, they'll hear you," someone nearby said.

But the man saw no reason to remain still. "Invader, what do you want from us?" he shouted when the Regent's huge form appeared in the doorway.

The Invid looked down at them, his antennae throbbing and hood puffed up. "You know very well what I want— the Flower of Life." He reached out and plucked the man from the crowd, his four-fingered hand fully encompassing the man's head. "Tell me where it is."

"Never—"

"You fool," the Regent rasped as he lifted the man to shoulder height, applying pressure as he dangled him over the screaming prisoners. The man's hands flailed wildly against the Regent's grip. "Where are the Flowers?"

The Tiresian's responses were muffled, panicked. "We don't know—"

"Tell me, you insignificant little worm!" the Regent said, and crushed the man's skull.

"We know nothing," someone in the crowd shouted. "The Masters never told us of such things!"

"My friend, I believe you," the Regent said after a moment. He released the now lifeless body. "Enforcer," he added, turning aside, "reward these creatures for their honesty."

The lieutenant stiffened. "At once, my lord." While the Regent exited the hall, the enforcer armed a spherical device and tossed it over his shoulder before the doors shut, sealing the prisoners inside.

An old man caught the device and sadly regarded its flashing lights. "What does it mean?" someone asked in a horror-stricken voice.

The old man forced himself to swallow. "It means our doom," he said softly.

The explosion took most of the temple with it.

Returned to his flagship, the Regent met with his scientists. They were barefoot beings much like himself, although no taller than the soldiers, dressed in unadorned white trousers and sashed jackets suggestive of oriental robes. In the presence of their king, they kept their arms folded across their chests, hands tucked inside jacket cuffs.

"Tell me what you know," the Regent asked them, despondent after this brief visit to Tirol's surface. "Is this moon as worthless as it seems?"

"We have yet to find any trace of the Flower," their spokesman said in a modulated voice. "And most of the population is too old and sickly to serve as slave labor. I'm afraid there is very little of use to us here."

"Perhaps it will simply take more digging to find what we seek. Come," the Regent instructed their overseer, Obsim, "there is something I wish to discuss with you."

As they walked—through an enormous hold lined top to bottom with Shock Troopers, Pincer and Command ships, and inward toward the very heart of the flagship— the Regent explained his position.

"Just because the Regis is somewhat more *evolved* than I am, she treats me like I just crawled from the swamp. I fear she'll try to undermine my authority; that's why this mission *must* succeed."

"I understand," Obsim said.

"I'm placing you in charge of the search on Tirol. The Inorganics will be your eyes and ears. Use them to uncover the secrets of this place."

Obsim inclined his head in a bow. "If this world holds

any clue to the matrix's whereabouts, I will find it."

"See that you do," the Regent added ominously.

A transparent transport tube conveyed them weight-lessly to the upper levels of the ship, where the Invid brain was temporarily housed. The brain was just that, a tower-ing fissured and convoluted organ of Protoculture instru-mentality enclosed in a hundred-foot-high bubble chamber filled with clear liquid.

The Regent's attempt to emulate the Masters' Protocul-ture Caps: his living computer.

King and scientist stood at the chamber's pulsating, bubbled base.

"The invasion is complete," the Regent directed up to the brain. "I have brought Tirol to its knees."

A synaptic dazzle spread across the underside of the instrument brain, tickling what might have been the pitui-tary body, the pons varolii, and corpora albicantia. The brain spoke. "And yet your search for the matrix con-tinues."

"For a while longer, yes," the Regent confirmed in de-fense of his actions, the chamber effervescence reflected in his glossy black eyes.

"Find Zor's ship and you will have what you seek. Not until then." The brain seemed to aspirate its words, sucking them in so that its speech resembled a tape played in re-verse.

"You've been talking to the Regis again!" the Regent growled. "You expect me to search for a ship that could be halfway across the galaxy?"

"Calculations suggest that such a journey would consti-tute a minor drain on existing Protoculture reserves when compared to these continued assaults against the Masters' realms."

"That may very well be," the Regent was willing to concede, "but conquest is growth. *Conquest* is evolvement!" He turned to Obsim. "My orders stand: section the brain. Transport the cutting to the surface to guide the Inorganics. Bring me what I seek and I will make you master of your own world. Fail, and I will leave you to rot on this ball of dust for an eternity."

■ ■■ ■ ■■ ■ ■■ ■■ ■■ ■ ■■ ■ ■■ ■ ■■ ■ ■■ ■ ■■ ■

CHAPTER
FIVE

*What with all the major players from the RDF and the South-
ern Cross in attendance [at the Hunters' wedding], one would
have expected at least one newsworthy incident; but in fact the
only negative scene was one touched off by Lynn-Minmei's song,
which provoked exclamations of disapproval from a few members
of the Sisterhood Society. "We'll be together," the chorus went,
"as married man and wife." Here was Lisa Hayes, first officer of
the SDFs 1 and 2, admiral of the fleet, and commander of the
entire SDF-3, suddenly reduced by Minmei's lyric to Rick Hunter's
wife!*

Footnote in *Fulcrum: Commentaries on the Second
Robotech War* by Major Alice Harper Argus (ret.)

RICK WATCHED THE EARTH AS IT SWUNG INTO VIEW
feeling a little like he imagined the starchild did in that old
science fiction classic. He knew it was stretching things a
bit to feel that way, but in a very real sense the future of the
planet was in the hands of a council of ordinary men and
women. *Human* beings, not superheroes or protectors, or
starchildren who had already crossed over.

Earth looked unchanged from up here, its recent scars
and still-open wounds concealed by a mantle of white
swirls and dense fronts. But Rick had walked Earth's
scorched surface for six years and knew the truth: his world
would never be the same. And it took a new kind of

strength to accept this fact, to overcome the inertia of age and surrender a host of childhood dreams.

"Penny for your thoughts," Lisa said from behind him.

He hadn't heard her enter, and swung around from the viewport with a guilty look on his face.

"Am I interrupting something?"

He smiled at her and shook his head. "A penny, huh . . . Is that all they're worth?"

"A nickel, then."

She came over to kiss him, and immediately sensed his remoteness. He turned back to the view as she released him. Sunlight touched the wingtips of dozens of shuttles ferrying guests up to the satellite for the wedding.

" 'The stars my destination,' " he mused. "I can't help wondering if we've made the right choice. It's like a crazy dream."

Lisa pursed her lips and nodded; Max had prepared her for Rick's mood, and she wanted him to understand that her shoulder was the softest around. Still, she didn't like his waffling and sudden indecisiveness. "It's not a crazy dream," she told him. "If we succeed, we'll be insuring a future for ourselves."

"I know, I know," he said dismissively. "I'm not as mixed up as I sound. It's just coming down so fast all of a sudden. The mission, our wedding . . ."

"We've had six years to think about this, Rick."

Rick took her in his arms; she linked her hands behind his neck. "I'm an idiot."

"Only if you're having doubts about us, Rick."

"Not now," he said, collecting on the kiss Max had interrupted earlier.

In his small cabinspace aboard the SDF-3, Jack Baker was softly thumping his head against a computer console.

There was just *too much to learn*. Not only did you have to prove yourself in air combat maneuvers, you had to know all this extra *stuff*! Ordnance specifications, drill procedures, TO&E nonsense, *Zentraedi*! for crying out loud . . . If he'd known that mecha piloting was going to involve all this, he would have just gone to college or something!

The computer sounded a tone, urging him to enter his response to the question it had flashed on the screen.

"Plot a course from *A* to *B*," Jack read, "taking into consideration vector variants listed above . . ." Jack scanned the tables hopelessly and bellowed a curse at the ceiling.

At the same moment, the cabin door hissed open and a VT lieutenant walked in. He took a long analytical look at Jack, then glanced at the monitor screen.

"Troubles, Baker?" he said, barely suppressing a grin.

Jack reached over and switched off the monitor. "No, no troubles."

The pilot sniggered. "Here, this oughta cheer you up."

Jack took the envelope and opened it: inside was a handwritten note from Admiral Hunter inviting him to the wedding reception. "'I hope you can make it,'" Jack read aloud three times, trying to convince himself that the note was on the level.

"From Richard A. Hunter," Jack said to the pilot, gloating. "My buddy, the admiral."

The hold chosen for the wedding was on the factory's upper level, where a massive overhead viewport had recently been installed expressly for the event. The space could accommodate several thousand, but by three o'clock on the afternoon of the big day every seat was filled. Rick and Lisa had demanded a simple ceremony nonetheless, and in keeping with their wishes the hold was minimally outfitted. Two tiered banks of chairs had been set up to face a raised platform, behind which rose a screen adorned with a large stylized cross. The stage was carpeted and matched by a five-hundred-foot-long red runner that covered the center aisle. Large floral arrangements had been placed along the aisle and perimeter of the stage, and in the hold beyond sat two rows of gleaming Alpha Veritechs, red on the right, blue on the left.

The front rows had been reserved for close friends and VIPs, who sat there now in their finest gowns, pleated uniforms, service ribbons, and golden-epauletted dress blues. The hold was humming with hundreds of individual conversations, and organ music was wafting from a dozen theater speakers. Bowie and Dana, who were supposed to be waiting with the wedding party, were playing a game of tag among the rows, and Jean Grant was chasing both of them, asking her son if was too much to request that he behave himself just this once.

"Can't you act like a grown-up!" she screamed, at the end of her rope.

"But I can't, Mom," the youngster returned to the amusement of everyone within earshot, "I've got the mind of a seven-year-old!"

Seating hadn't been prearranged along any "familial" lines, but a curious breakdown had begun from the start. On one side sat Field Marshal Anatole Leonard and most of the Southern Cross apparat—T. R. Edwards, Dr. Lazlo Zand, Senator Wyatt Moran, and dozens of lesser officers and dignitaries—and on the other, the RDF contingent: Vince and Jean Grant, Miriya Sterling, Drs. Lang and Penn and the rest of the Plenipotentiary Council, Jonathan Wolff, the Emersons, and others. In a tight-knit group behind the council members sat Exedore, and Dana Sterling's three deathly-ill Zentraedi godfathers, Rico, Konda, and Bron. Breetai's micronized troops were farther back, along with some of the Wolff Pack, the Skull and Ghost Squadrons.

Up front, on the sunny side, were Lynn-Minmei and her singing partner, Janice Em. Lisa's response to Minmei's offer that day in the gown shop had been straightforward: she had asked her to sing at the wedding.

Janice Em was something of an enigma to the media. Word had it that she was Dr. Lang's niece, but rumor linked her to the wizard of Robotechnology in more intimate terms. In any case, she seemed to have appeared on the scene out of nowhere two years earlier, only to become Lynn-Minmei's much needed tenor and constant companion. She was a few inches taller than Minmei, with large blue eyes set in a somewhat pale but attractive face. Her hair color changed every few months, but today it was a delicate lavender, pulled back in a rose clasp behind one ear. She had chosen a yellow spaghetti-strapped gown to complement Minmei's blue halter and offset it with a necklace of ancient Egyptian turquoise.

"Did I ever tell you about the time Rick and I got married?" Minmei was saying just now.

Janice heard the sadness in Minmei's voice, but chose to react to the statement. "Maybe you should be telling Lisa," she suggested. "Or are you saving it for when the chaplain asks if anyone can show 'just cause'?"

Minmei reacted as though she had been slapped; then she let out her breath and laughed. It was so typically *Janice* to say something like that. When the press grilled her for the scoop on Janice and Dr. Lang, Minmei would often reply,"Well, if she's not related to him, she's certainly got his sense of humor."

"It was a fantasy wedding, Janice," Minmei explained. "When we were trapped together in a hold in the SDF-1."

"And here you are trapped with him in another hold."

Minmei ignored it. "I just can't stop myself from think-ing about what might have been."

"'The saddest are: it might have been,'" Janice quoted. "But forget it, Lynn. The past is only an arrangement of photons receding at lightspeed."

"That's very romantic, Janice."

"Romance is for storytellers."

"And what about our songs—you don't call them ro-mantic?"

Janice turned to her straight-faced. "Our songs are weapons."

Above the would-be chapel, on an observation balcony Max had christened the "ready-reaction room," Rick stood in front of a mirror trying to tie a knot. His tux was white with sky-blue lapels.

"The balloon's about to go up," Max enthused, bursting in on him.

"I can't do it, Max. You're going to have to do it for me."

It took Max a moment to understand that Rick was re-ferring to the tie; he breathed a sigh of relief and went over to his friend. "Here, I'm an expert with these things."

Rick inclined his head to the view below while Max went to work on the tie. He felt as though his stomach had reconfigured itself to some entirely new mode.

"There," Max said. "It's a matter of finesse."

Rick thanked him. "A man couldn't have a finer best man or best friend. I mean that."

Max blushed. "Hey, I was saving that for the toast."

"Okay," Rick said in a determined voice. "Let's move."

He reached up to give a final adjustment to the tie only to have it slip and loosen up.

Max looked at it and shrugged. "Well, maybe you'll start a trend."

In the end you go it alone, Rick was saying to himself ten minutes later as he turned to watch Lisa come down the aisle. Breetai, in his helmet-mask and Ironman getup walked beside her, and Rick couldn't help seeing them as some kind of whacko father-and-daughter tag-team couple. Max's daughter was one step behind them. But as Lisa drew nearer the image left him, and so did the nervousness. She had roses and baby's breath in her hair, a choker of real pearls, and she looked radiant. Behind Lisa's back, Dana made a face at ringbearer Bowie and curled her fingers at her mom.

Max and Breetai left the platform soon after, and the chaplain began to read the short service Lisa had written. A few minutes later Rick and Lisa were joining hands, exchanging rings and vows, and suddenly it was over.

Or just beginning.

They kissed and a thousand strobe lights flashed. Cheers and applause rose from the crowd above a flourish of strings and horns; and outside the viewport, teams of Veritechs completed a series of slow-mo formation flybys. A fanfare sounded as local space came to life with starbursts, roostertails, and fountains of brilliant color.

Rick and Lisa shook a thousand hands and kissed a thousand cheeks; then they danced together to Minmei and Janice's song. Spotlights found them in the hold as they moved through gentle arcs and twirls across the floor. Rick held her lovingly and caught the glint of teardrops in the corner of her eyes. He squeezed her hand and felt a wave

of sadness wash through him. It was the song perhaps, a
love song to be sure, but one sung with a sense of implied
loss, an awareness of the ephemeral nature of all things.

> A world turns to the edge of night,
> the moon and stars so very bright;
> your face glows in the candlelight,
> it's all because tonight's the night . . .
> Now hold my hand and take this ring
> as we unite in harmony.
> We can begin to live the dream,
> the dream that's meant for you and me.
>
> To be together,
> For the first time in our lives,
> it's us together.
> As married man and wife, we'll be together
> from now on, until death do us part;
> and even then, I hope our love lasts forever.

"Oh, Rick," Lisa whispered in his ear, moved to tears
by the Voice that had conquered an army. "How I wish
Claudia and Roy could be here."

Rick led her through a turn that kept her back to the
guests. *And Ben*, he thought. *And Gloval and Sammie and
Vanessa and Kim and the countless millions sacrificed to
war's insatiable thirst . . .*

> I promise to be always true
> until the very end's in view.
> In good times and the bad times, too,
> I know that we can make it through.
> As one united we'll be strong;
> because together we belong.

If I could sing to you a song,
I'd sing of love that won't go wrong.

If we're together,
we'll make a brand new life for us together,
as married man and wife, we'll stay together...

Couples began to join them on the dance floor, and
when the song finished, the party began in earnest. Hap-
pily, Rick found himself with some free moments while
Lisa was off circulating table to table. Oddly enough,
members of the Southern Cross and RDF were mingling
without incident, and everywhere Rick looked he saw people having a good time. Except perhaps for Jean Grant,
who was looking a little frazzled after having spent most of
the ceremony chasing Bowie and Dana around.

A photographer brought Rick and Lisa back together for
the cake cutting, but Rick drew the line at that, and refused
to take part in any of the archaic dances the band insisted
on playing. Instead, he wandered around with a smile frozen in place that misrepresented his true inner state. He had
realized, as though waking from a dream, that there was
only the mission now. No wedding to absorb his concerns,
no higher priority than the SDF-3 and his command.

It was a frightening realization.

Elsewhere, Jonathan Wolff was zeroing in on Minmei.

"This has got to be the biggest reception I've ever
played," Minmei was exclaiming to Janice as Wolff came
over.

"You sang beautifully," he began on a confident note.

Minmei recognized a certain look in his eye and began

to glance around for an escape route. "Uh, thank you," she said in a distracted way.

"The name's Wolff. And do you know how long I've wanted to meet you?"

Wolff! Oh, terrific, Minmei was saying to herself, when Janice suddenly blurted out, "Try humming a few bars."

Wolff's smile collapsed and he began to look back and forth between the two women uncertainly. "I, uh—"

"Oh, right, you were talking to Minmei, not me," Janice said. "Look, I'll relocate and you can give it a second try."

Minmei and Wolff watched her walk off.

"Don't mind Janice, she's got a very peculiar sense of humor."

Wolff cleared his throat meaningfully and was about to say something, but Minmei excused herself and wandered away.

"There's someone over there I want to talk to," she said over her shoulder.

Undaunted, Wolff straightened his torso harness—in case anyone was watching. He saw Minmei talking to Exedore and three other Zentraedi men. But then Wolff noticed something else: a man about his own age standing nearby was also watching Minmei. Watching her with an almost palpable intensity. Wolff repositioned himself for a better view of the stranger, a maintenance tech by the look of his uniform. But there was something disturbingly familiar about him. Wolff was sure he had never met the man, but was equally certain he had seen him somewhere. As he studied the man's tall, lean figure and bearded face, an image began to form. The beard would have to go, Wolff decided, and the hair would have to be a lot longer and darker . . . But *where* had he seen him—in the Control

Zone, maybe—and why did martial arts and old movies come to mind?

Karen Penn, her father, and Dr. Lang were eating slices of wedding cake when a slovenly-dressed civilian joined them at the table. Lang introduced Karen to Dr. Lazlo Zand, a cold-handed man with eyes as pupilless as Lang's own.

"Good to meet you," Karen said, forcing a smile and wondering if Zand ran on ice water.

"Charmed," he returned. "That blond hair. You remind me of little Dana."

Karen felt a chill run through her, and something seemed to make her fork leap from the plate. She bent to retrieve it, but someone had beat her to it.

"Allow me," a red-haired ensign told her. "I'm pretty handy with hardware."

"Karen, Ensign . . . Baker, if I'm not mistaken," offered Lang.

She and Baker were both still holding on to the fork and locked in on each other's eyes.

"The pleasure's at least fifty percent mine." Baker smiled. He let go of the fork. "Consider me at your service, ma'am."

Karen's eyebrows went up. "I'll keep it in mind."

"And I'll keep *you* in mind," Baker said, excusing himself and moving off.

"Bit of a hotshot," commented Lang.

"That's the sort of person you'll be wasting your time with from now on," Harry Penn added gruffly.

Karen smiled. "I'm not so sure about that, Dad."

"But your father's right," Zand interjected, narrowing his eyes. "Scientists are more fun."

Karen couldn't hold the man's gaze. Absently, she tried

to raise a forkful of cake to her mouth. The utensil was twisted beyond recognition.

The party was still cooking eight hours later, but Rick and Lisa were ready to call it a day. They said their farewells from the balcony overlooking the hold; and Lisa got ready to give the bridal bouquet a healthy send-off.

At the last minute, Janice had thrust Minmei into the midst of the crowd of eligible women, but had herself taken off for parts unknown. Now Minmei was pressed tight in the center of that mass of supercharged youth, surrounded by officers, enlisted-rating techs, and cadets, most of whom were younger than she was. One honey-blond-haired ensign to her left couldn't have been more than seventeen.

On the balcony, Lisa was warning that anyone who hoped to remain single should stay out of the line of fire. Then she gave the thing a windup underhanded toss, and Minmei saw it coming.

She barely had to stretch out her hands, and what was stranger still, the women around her seemed *to give it to her*.

"See you all after the honeymoon," Lisa shouted, perhaps unaware of the bouquet's landing zone.

"Yeah, in about eight hours from now!" Rick added, tugging his bride away.

Minmei lowered her face into the flowers, then gave her head a quick shake when she looked up. *It's over*, she thought, recalling a sad song she used to sing. *Now I've got to get on with my life*.

"Good-bye, Rick," she said softly. *It is you I still see . . .*

* * *

On Optera, the Invid Regis learned of her husband's
imminent return and made immediate plans to leave the
planet. She didn't delude herself with thoughts that this
might be some trial separation. Of course, it meant aban-
doning all the Genesis Pit experiments in evolution she had
begun here, her progress in the Great Work of transmutation and freedom from the *base condition*; but what strides
could she hope to make in his presence, what chance did
she have to fulfill herself? No, he had held her back long
enough. Further, it meant that she would have to decide
what constituted a just division of their resources. He already had the living computer; but there were other Protoculture instrumentalities that would serve her as well as the
brain once had. And she would take along half her active
children, but leave him that sleeping brood she had not yet
seen fit to awaken.

Their home on Optera, their *castle*, was an enormous
hemispherical hive, once the sacred inverted chalice of the
Great Work, but now a profane *dwelling* filled with his
things—his servants and ridiculous possessions. He had
claimed to be doing all this for her sake, and for a time she
could almost believe him, pitiful as his attempts were. But
she soon realized that he was merely nurturing himself with
these conquests and acquisitive drives.

The Regent's ignorance and stubbornness had been
enough to drive her mad. He was in every way her intellec-
tual and spiritual inferior; and yet his will was powerful,
and in his presence she could feel his sick mind reaching
out for her, trying to smother her. She was certain that
unless she left Optera, he would one day succeed in drag-
ging her down to his barbaric level.

But she was free of him now, her mind clear on the path
she had to take. No longer subservient to his dark demands, she would strike out on her own. If the matrix was

to be found, it was she who would find it. Not by sanitizing the Masters' insignificant worlds, but by sending out her sensor nebulae to the far reaches of the galaxy to locate Zor's dimensional fortress. Then she would take the Flowers back from the thieves who had stolen them; she would liberate them from their matrix prison and find a new Optera for her experiments!

In the meantime the planet Praxis would suffice.

And woe to any who would stand in her way!

CHAPTER
SIX

Actually, I've been thinking about it for months now, but I just didn't know how to ask, and I wasn't sure if you would understand my decision. Could you see me walking up to Lang or one of those council stiffs and saying, "Uh, do you think I might be able to go along on the ride?" And then have to tell you that I was going to be doing a tour by myself this time. Taking my act to Tirol—you would have brained me. I hope you'll forgive me, and I want you to know that we'll pick up right where we left off when the Expeditionary mission returns. I mean, who knows, maybe I'll have added a bunch of new stuff to our repetoire. Anyway, I'm certain the experience will be good for me.

Lynn-Minmei's good-bye note to her manager,
Samson "Sharky" O'Toole

THE ALARM WENT OFF AT 5:15 A.M. "RISE AND SHINE," said a synthesized, possibly female voice from the room's control deck.

Rick pulled the sheet over his head and buried his face in the pillow. He could sense Lisa stirring beside him, sitting up and stretching. In a moment he felt her warm hand on his bare back.

"Morning."

"What good is it being an admiral if you can't sleep late?" he asked without lifting his head.

She laughed and kissed the nape of his neck. "Not today, Rick."

"Then tell me why five-fifteen never seemed this early before."

"Maybe because bed never felt this good before," she purred, snuggling against his back.

Rick rolled over and put his arms around her. "That's a fact, ma'am."

The door tone sounded, ending their embrace. Rick muttered something and climbed out of bed, stepping into trousers before answering the door.

"Good morning, Mr. and Mrs. Hunter," a robo-butler announced. The thing was squat and silly-looking, with a rubber skirt that concealed its wheels; it was holding a full breakfast tray in its plasticized grips. "Dr. Lang wanted you to have breakfast in bed," the butler continued in the same monotone. "Please enter the appropriate commands."

Rick allowed the piece of Robowizardry to enter, but shut it down soon afterward, taking over the butler's program and conveying the tray to bed himself.

He bowed theatrically as Lisa sat up. "Service with a genuine smile."

They ate hurriedly and said little, famished all of a sudden. Then they showered together and began to dress. Rick watched Lisa in front of the mirror, smoothing her uniform and adjusting the collar of her jacket.

"Off to work," he said, looking himself over. "Do you realize that the next time we're in this room together, I'll be asking you what you did today, and you'll tell me that you commanded a starship across the galaxy. Does that sound a little *odd* to you?"

"Odd how?" she said, with a crooked smile.

"Odd like not something we do every day."

Lisa came over to tug his black torso harness into place. "Just think of it as a honeymoon."

Rick made a face. "I'll be sure and tell that to the Masters."

Jean Grant had cried at the wedding; those, however, had been tears of joy and remembrance, while the ones streaming down her cheeks today were anything but. Bowie was on the verge of tears himself, but was trying hard to be a *man about it*. Not that mom and son stood out any, though; the shuttle hold was filled with like scenes: tears, embraces, heartfelt exchanges. Wedding guests and family members would be shuttled home over the course of the next few days, but with the SDF-3 launch window less than four hours off, this was the crew's last chance for good-byes. Within a month, Human factory personnel would be transferred to new assignments on-planet, or at Moon Base or Liberty Space Station. No decision had been made concerning the satellite itself, but speculation was that the Zentraedi crew would remove the installation from Earth orbit—to where, no one knew.

Vince Grant bent down and put a hand on his son's head, giving it an affectionate rub. "It's going to be all right, Bowie. We'll be back before you know it."

"But why can't I come with you?" he wanted to know. "Other kids are going—kids not too much older than us," he added, including Dana. Bowie was thinking of one kid in particular he had met at the wedding, Dr. Lang's godson, Scott Bernard.

"That's true, sweetie," Jean said, smiling through her tears. "But you know you can't go." She touched Bowie's chest with her fingertips. "Your heart won't let you go."

Dana, who was bored and practicing spin kicks against a bulkhead, frowned and said, "Come on, Bowie. We don't want to go with them anyway. Space is no fun, anybody knows that."

Max and Miriya regarded each other and shook their heads as if to say, *where* did that one come from?

"Dana's right, Bowie," Jean smiled, tugging in a sob. "It isn't going to be any fun."

"Yeah, Dana, but you were in space already," Bowie pointed out. "*I've* never been there."

Rolf Emerson took advantage of a momentary silence to step forward and put his arm around the boy. "We're going to have a good time, Bowie. You wait and see."

Vince and Jean embraced Rolf. "Take good care of him for us, Rolf," Vince said with a serious look.

"You know I will."

Just then Lazlo Zand walked by headed for the shuttle ramp. Instinctively, Emerson hugged Dana and Bowie to his legs, a look in his dark eyes like he wanted to put a stake through Zand's heart.

Elsewhere in the shuttle boarding area, Janice and Minmei had received their seat assignments and were walking off in the direction of the VIP lounge. They were ordinary folk this morning, dressed in slacks and simple blouses. There was plenty of time to kill until the prep call, and Minmei wanted to get a drink.

"What's with you today?" Janice asked while they moved through the crowd. "The clouds are below us, so I don't see how you can have your head in them." When Minmei didn't respond, Janice took her by the arm. "Earth calling Lynn-Minmei. Please relay your hyperspace coordinates."

"Huh?" Minmei said, turning to her.

Janice made an exasperated sound. "What is it—Rick?"

Minmei looked away. "He always looked out for me. I just don't know if I can leave him like this."

"Look, Lynn," Janice began in a worried voice, "I don't

think Lisa is going to appreciate your cutting into their—"

"If I could just see him once more. *Both* of them. Only to wish them good luck."

"You already did that—about two dozen times!"

Janice could see that she wasn't listening; Minmei's eyes were searching the bay for something. "There!" she said after a moment, pointing to a small EVA vehicle near a secondary launch port reserved for maintenance craft.

"I'm afraid to ask," Janice said warily. But Minmei was already on her way.

"Admiral on the bridge!" a young enlisted-rating tech announced, snapping to as Lisa stepped through the hatch. She couldn't help remembering Captain Gloval constantly smacking his head on a hatch very similar to this one. And indeed he would have felt right at home on the SDF 3 bridge, which for all intents and purposes was identical to that on the SDF-1. Lisa had insisted it be so, even though Lang had tried to convince her of the giant strides his teams had made since reconstructing that doomed fortress. There were redundancies and severe limitations to the design, he had argued; but in the end Lisa had her way. It was her command, and this bridge was as much a tribute as anything else. To Gloval, to Claudia and the others . . . Of course, there were *some* changes that had to be allowed. The crew, for example: they were all men.

"At ease, gentlemen," Lisa told them.

She led herself through a tour of the now completed room, running her hands across the consoles and acceleration seats. Along the rear bulkhead were two four-by-four monitor screens linked to internal systemry and astrogation. Starboard was a complex laser communication and scanner console, crowned by a tall multiscreened threat board. And forward, below a wraparound forward viewport, were twin duty stations like the ones she and Claudia had manned for almost three years.

Lisa shook hands with her exec and crew—Forsythe, Blake, Colton and the rest. It was a formality, given the fact they all knew one another, but a necessary one. She wished each man good luck, then moved toward the raised command chair that was hers alone. She took a long time settling into its padded seat, but why not: the moment was six years in the making.

A terrible memory of her last short-lived command flashed through her mind, but she willed it away. She took a lingering glance around the room and declared in a determined voice, "Mister Blake, I want systems status."

If Lisa's new space was compact, tidy, and familiar, Rick's was large and impersonal. Constructed concurrently with its Earthside counterpart, the command, control, and communications center was an enormous room more than two hundred feet square and almost half as high. A fifty-by-fifty-foot screen dominated the bulkhead opposite Rick's command balcony with its half-dozen consoles and monitors. Below, a horizontal position board was surrounded by more than twenty individual duty stations, and adjacent to this forward, a bank of as many stations tied to the central display screen. Along the port bulkhead were peripheral screens, tech stations, and banks of sophisticated instrumentality, with a great Medusa's head of cables, feeders, and power relays running floor to ceiling.

"Quite a sight, isn't it, Admiral?" said someone off to Rick's right.

Rick turned, aware that he had been staring open-mouthed at the room, and found T. R. Edwards regarding him analytically from the command balcony railing. "Uh, impressive," Rick returned, underplaying his amazement.

He had of course been here often enough, but still struggled in unguarded moments with the enormity of his responsibility.

"'Impressive.'" Edwards laughed, approaching Rick now. "Interesting choice. I think I would have said 'awesome,' or 'incredible,' or even 'magnificent.' But then, I didn't spend three years in space on the SDF-1, did I? Did you think the Grand Cannon *impressive*, Admiral? You did get to see it, didn't you?"

"Actually, I didn't, General," Rick said, wondering what Edwards was getting at. "I only saw it in ruins . . . where it belonged in the first place."

Edwards grinned. "Oh, of course. I forgot. *You* were the one who rescued the Hayes woman, uh, the admiral."

Rick caught a reflection of himself in Edwards's faceplate, then looked directly into Edwards's good eye. "Something bothering you, Edwards?"

Edwards took a step back, motioning to himself with elaborate innocence. "Me? Why, no, not at all. I suppose I'm just a bit overcome by this room of ours." Edwards folded his arms and stood at the rail, a prince on a battlement. He turned to Rick and grinned. "Has anyone ever had a finer War Room, Admiral?"

Rick's lips were a thin line. "I prefer Situation Room. I thought I made that clear at the briefings."

"Forgive me," Edwards said, throwing his hands out apologetically. "*Situation* Room." He swung round to the view again. "What an impressive Situation Room."

Belowdecks, Jack Baker cursed—the RDF, his commanders, his luck, himself ultimately. *It was because of that oversight in the simulator*, he decided. *That* was what had done it, that was what had turned off Hunter and Sterling. A-and that handwritten invitation to the reception—

ha! Richard A. Hunter indeed. Richard Anti-Baker Hunter was more like it. Or why else wouldn't he have pulled the assignment he wanted? Skull Squadron . . . that was where the fun was. Even Ghost would've done the trick, although he did have some reservations about that General Edwards. But, *hell*! to be stuck with Commander Grant! Grant was all right, of course, but his unit was ground-based, for cry'nout loud. And what kind of action could a guy expect to see on land on a mission like this! And what was an *ensign* doing there? Temporary duty or not, it just didn't make any sense, no sense at all.

"I shoulda gone to college," Baker muttered as he shouldered his way through a group of enlisted ratings to report in.

Most of his Expeditionary Force mates in the mecha hangar were marveling at the two transports that were central to the battalion's strength—the GMU, and the drop-ship that conveyed it planetside—but to Jack the devices were just modular nightmares: overworked, underpowered, and unimportant. Veritechs were what made it happen. One pilot, one mecha. Plenty of speed, range, and firepower, and nothing to drag you down. *Nothing extraneous in mind or body*, as Jack was fond of quoting, often fantasizing about what those early Macross days must have been like, pushing the envelope and *azending*! *Yeah!*

These . . . *monstrosities*, on the other hand, were about as sleek as an old-fashioned tank. Course there were plenty of good things inside—Hovertanks, Logans, and such— but he would have to get himself transferred to the Wolff Pack if he ever hoped to ride one of those.

Jack decided to circle the GMU and see if he couldn't find something, *something* he could get excited about. The thing was huge, maybe five hundred feet long, with eight one-hundred-foot-high globular wheels affixed to massive transaxles, banks of superspot running lights, hidden particle-projection cannon turrets, and multiple-missile launch racks. Up front were two retractable off-loading ramps, and up top, behind blast deflectors, two external command stations positioned on either side of the unit's real prize: an enormous pulse-cannon, which, like a fire engine's tower ladder, could be raised and rotated.

Jack was still appraising the unit five minutes later when Karen Penn suddenly appeared on one of the ramp walkways. The body-hugging RDF jumpsuit did things for her figure that the dress hadn't, and Jack's scowl gave way to a wide-eyed look of enchantment.

Karen saw him, smiled, and waved. When she was within earshot she called brightly, "Hey, Baker, what are you doing here?"

Jack smiled back and cupped his hands to his mouth. "Luck of the draw!"

"I am beside myself," Dr. Lang confided to Exedore as the two men completed their prelaunch inspection of the fortress's spacefold generators and Reflex drives. They were the same ones that had once powered Breetai's flagship, but Lang's Robotechnicians had spiffed them up a bit. It had long been the professor's wish to cannibalize one of the spacefold generators just to take a peek at its Protoculture core, but he knew this would have to wait till a time when fold systemry could be spared. Presently, however, Protoculture remained the most precious substance in the universe, and Lang's teams had yet to discover the philosophers' stone that would enable them to create it. So chips and sealed generators were transferred intact from ship to ship or mecha to mecha. But even with all the energy cells the RDF had managed to salvage from the Zentraedi warships that had crashed on Earth, the supply was hardly inexhaustible.

How had Zor created the stuff? Lang was forever asking himself. He understood that it had something to do with the Flowers Exedore spoke of—the Flowers of Life. But Lang had never seen one, and how in any case had Zor gone from Flower to Protoculture? It was one of the many questions he hoped the Masters would answer once peace negotiations were out of the way. And then there were all unresolved puzzles centering around Zor hims the time being Lang was content with his ow triumphs.

"It's more than I ever hoped for."

Exedore might have recognized the look on Lang's face as one often observed on the faces of children on Christmas mornings. The Zentraedi ambassador picked up on Lang's tone of anticipation as well.

"Well, can you imagine how I must feel, Doctor, to be going home after so many years?"

Lang looked at Exedore as though noticing something for the first time. "Yes, yes, I see what you mean, my friend. And in a strange way I, too, feel as if I'm returning home."

Exedore thought he grasped Lang's meaning, and shook his head. "No, Doctor. You will see that Tirol is not for you. Earth is your home, and ever shall be."

"Perhaps," Lang said with a glint in his eye. "But we have seen more radical reshapings in the past few years, have we not?"

Exedore was about to reply when a tech interrupted the conversation to inform Lang that all systems were go and the bridge was awaiting confirmation.

"Well, give the admiral what she wants, Mr. Price," Lang declared. "The moment has arrived."

A murmur of excitement swept through the crowds waiting in the shuttle boarding area. Suddenly people were moving in haste toward the viewports and breaking into spontaneous applause.

"Now's our chance!" Minmei said over her shoulder to Janice.

From the forward seat of the EVA craft where she and Janice had been hiding for the past few hours, Minmei could just discern the rounded, main-gun booms of the SDF-3 nosing into view from the satellite's null-gee construction hold.

"Now, Janice, now!" Minmei urged.

Janice bit her lower lip and began to activate a series of switches across the craft's instrument panel. Displays came to life one by one, suffusing the small cockpit with whirring sounds and comforting amber light. Abruptly, the small ship lurched forward as a conveyor carried it toward the launch bay.

Minmei searched for some indication that they had been spotted, but it appeared that even the techs' attention had been diverted by the unannounced emergence of the fortress. And before she could complete the silent prayer she had begun, the craft was lauched.

Minmei had nothing but confidence in her partner's ability to pilot the craft and position it in close proximity to the SDF-3; she had seen Janice do far more amazing things during their two-year friendship.

She frequently recalled the first time Dr. Lang had introduced her to Janice. He talked about Janice as though she were God's gift to the world; and later on Minmei under-

stood that Lang's hyperboles were not so far off the mark.
Minmei felt that Janice was somewhat cool and remote—
the only man in her life was that Senator Moran, and it
seemed a strange sort of relationship—but Janice could
fly, fight, absorb, and retain incredible amounts of information, speak a dozen languages, including Zentraedi. Her
considerable talents notwithstanding, however, it was Janice's *voice* that Lang had raved about; about how she and
Minmei could complement each other in the most perfect
way imaginable. And not solely for purposes of entertain-
ment. What Minmei's voice had achieved with the Zentraedi, Minmei and Janice's combined voice could replicate
tenfold. And should the Robotech Masters decide to send a
new wave of bio-engineered warriors to Earth in the
SDF-3's absence, that *defensive harmony* might very well
prove the planet's saving grace.

Our songs are weapons, Minmei heard Janice saying.

Minmei was no stranger to grandiose dreams or grandiose purpose, and she had readily agreed to keep Lang's
secret. Janice, too, agreed, and the two women had become close friends as well as partners. But after two years
of that, dreams were suddenly a new priority, and Lang's
concerns seemed paranoid now. So as the EVA craft began
to approach the slow-moving fortress, Minmei told Janice
to hold to a parallel course.

"But we can't remain here, Lynn. The ship is going to
fold in a matter of minutes."

"Just do it for me, please, Janice."

Janice was quiet for a moment; then she said, "You have
no plans of returning to the satellite, do you?"

Minmei swung around in her seat and reached for her
friend's hand. "Are you with me?"

Janice saw the commingling of fear and desperation in
Minmei's blue eyes, and smiled. "Do I have a choice?"

Minmei looked down on Earth's oceans and clouds, and completed her prayer.

"Engineering confirms attainment lunar orbit," Blake updated. "We are go for launch, Admiral."

Lisa turned in her chair to study a peripheral monitor screen. There was a steady bass rumbling through the entire ship that made it difficult to hear statements voiced on the bridge. But at the same time Lisa was aware of the background blare of klaxons and alert sirens ordering all hands to their launch stations.

"Mr. Colton, start your count," Lisa ordered, hands tight on the command chair's armrests.

"T-minus-ten and counting," Colton shouted above the roar and shudder.

"Nine . . ."

"Admiral!" Blake said suddenly. "I'm showing an unidentified radar blip well inside the fold zone!"

"Five, four . . ."

Lisa craned her neck around. "What is it?!"

"Ship, sir—EVA craft!"

"Two, one . . ."

"Too late!"

"Zero!"

"Execute!" Lisa shouted.

And the mile-long ship jumped.

While the life expectancy of a standard Zentraedi mecha pilot had been determined by the Robotech Masters at three years, the life expectancy of a comparable Invid pilot was never even addressed. In effect, all Invid troops (save the sexually-differentiated scientists) could be activated and deactivated at a moment's notice—initially by the Regis only, and later by the living computers the Queen Mother helped create to satisfy her husband's wounded pride (after the "affair" with Zor). . . . A self-generated variety of Protoculture was essential to mecha operation, in the form of a viscous green fluid that filled the cockpit space. It was through this nutrient bath (liquified fruits from the mature Optera plants) that the living computers, or "brains," communicated with the ranks.

Selig Kahler, *The Tirolian Campaign*

"**Y**ES, MY BOY, I'VE BEEN MEANING TO SHOW YOU this place for quite a long time," Cabell confessed, gesturing to the wonders of the subterranean chamber. The scientist and his apprentice were deep in the labyrinth beneath Tiresia's pyramidal Royal Hall. "A pity it has to be under these circumstances."

It was a laboratory and monitoring facility the likes of which Rem had never seen. There were wall-to-wall consoles and screens, networktops piled high with data cards and ancient print documents, and dozens of unidentifiable tools and devices. In the glow of the room's archaic illumination panels, the place had a dusty, unused look.

"And this was really *his* study?" Rem said in disbelief.

Cabell nodded absently, his thoughts on the Pollinators and what could be done with them now. The shaggy creatures had become quiet and docile all of a sudden, huddling together in a tight group in one corner of the room. It was as if they had instinctively located some sort of power spot. Cabell heard Rem gasp; the youth was staring transfixed at a holo-image of Zor he had managed to conjure up from one of the networks, the only such image left on Tirol.

"But . . . but this is *impossible*," Rem exclaimed. "We're identical!"

Cabell swallowed and found his voice. "Well, there's some resemblance, perhaps," he said, downplaying the likeness. "Something about the eyes and mouth . . . But switch that thing off, boy, we've got work to do."

Mystified, Rem did so, and began to clear a workspace on one of the countertops, while Cabell went around the room activating terminals and bringing some of the screens to life. The old man knew that he could communicate directly with the Elders from here, but there was no need for that yet. Instead, he set about busying himself with the transponder, and within an hour he had the data he needed to pinpoint the source of its power.

"As I thought," Cabell mused, as schematics scrolled across a screen. "They are almost directly above us in the Royal Hall. Apparently they've brought some sort of command center down from the fleet ships. Strange, though . . . the emanations are closer to organic than computer-generated."

"What does it mean?" Rem asked over Cabell's shoulder.

"That we now know where we must direct our strike." He had more to add, but autoactivation sounds had suddenly begun to fill the lab, drawing his attention to a screen off to his left, linked, Cabell realized, to one of Tirol's few remaining orbital scanners. And shortly, as a deepspace image formed on the screen, it was Cabell's turn to gasp.

"Oh, my boy, tell me I'm not seeing things!"

"It's a starship," Rem said, peering at the screen. "But it's not Invid, is it?"

Cabell had his palms pressed to his face in amazement. "Far from it, Rem, far from it . . . Don't you see?—it's *his* ship, Zor's!"

"But how, Cabell?"

Cabell shot to his feet. "The Zentraedi! They've recaptured it and returned." He put his hands on Rem's shoulders. "We're saved, my boy. Tirol is saved!"

But the moon's orbital watchdogs weren't the only scanners to have picked up on the ship. Inside the Royal Hall—converted by Enforcer units to an Invid headquarters—the slice of brain Obsim had transported to Tirol's surface began to speak.

"Intruder alert," the synthesized voice announced matter-of-factly. "An unidentified ship has just entered the Valivarre system on a course heading for Tirol. Estimated arrival time: one period."

The cerebral scion approximated the appearance of the Regent's living computer, and floated in a tall, clear fluid bubble chamber that was set into an hourglass-shaped base.

"Identify and advise," Obsim ordered.

"Searching . . ."

The Invid scientist turned his attention to a spherical, geodesiclike communicator, waiting for an image to form.

"Insufficient data for unequivocal identification."

"Compare and approximate."

"*Quiltra Quelamitzs*," the computer responded a moment later. A deepspace view of the approaching ship appeared in the sphere, and alongside it the various memory profiles the brain had employed in its search.

"Identify."

"Zentraedi battlecruiser."

Obsim's snout sensors twitched and blanched. *The Zentraedi*, he thought, *after all these generations, returned to their home system*. He could only hope they were an advance group for the Masters themselves, for that would mean a return of the Flower, the return of hope . . .

He instructed the computer to alert all troopship commanders immediately. "Stand by to assault."

Much as spacefold was a warping of the continuum, it was a mind-bending experience as well. The world was filled with a thousand voices speaking at once, and dreamtime images of externalized selves loosed to live out an array of parallel moments, each as real and tangible as the next, each receding as swiftly as it was given birth. The stars would shimmer, fade, and emerge reassembled. Light and shadow reversed. Space was an argent sea or sky shot through with an infinite number of black holes, smeared with smoky nebulae.

This marked Lisa's sixth jump, but familiarity did nothing to lessen the impact of hyperspace travel, the SDF-3's tunnel in the sky. It felt as though she had awakened not on the other side of the galaxy but on the other side of a dream, somehow exchanged places with her nighttime self, so that it was her *doppelgänger* who sat in the command chair now. Voices from the bridge crew surfaced slowly, muffled and unreal, as if from a great depth.

". . . reports entry to Valivarre system."

"Systems status," she said weakly and by rote. "Secure from launch stations."

Some of the techs came to even more slowly than she did, bending to their tasks as though exhausted.

"All systems check out, Admiral. Dr. Lang is on-screen."

Lisa glanced up at the monitor just as the doctor was offering his congratulations. "I've taken the liberty of ordering course and velocity corrections. Hope you don't mind, Lisa."

Lang seemed unfazed by their transit through hyperspace; it was one of the strange things about a jump: like altitude sickness, there was no way to predict who would and would not suffer side effects. She was certain that a number of the crew were already being removed to sick bay. Surprised at her own state of well-being, Lisa shook her head and smiled. "We've made it, then, we've actually made it?"

"See for yourself," Lang said.

Lisa swung to study a screen, and there it was: a magnified crescent of the ringed and marbled jadelike giant, with its distant primary peeking into view—a magnesium-white jewel set on the planet's rim. A schematic of the system began to take shape, graphics highlighting one of Fantoma's dozen moons and enlarging it, as analytical readouts scrolled across an ancillary screen.

"Tirol," said Lisa. The moon was closing on Fantoma's darkside. Then, with a sinking feeling, she recalled the EVA blip.

"Still with us," a tech reported in an anxious tone. "But we're leaving it farther behind every second."

"Dr. Lang," Lisa started to say. But all at once alert signals were flashing all over the bridge.

"Picking up multiple radar signals, sir. Approach vectors coming in . . ."

Lisa's eyes went wide. "Sound general quarters. Go to high alert and open up the com net. And get me Admiral Hunter—*immediately.*"

"We've got them," Rick was saying a moment later from a screen.

"Do we have a signature?" Lisa asked the threat-board tech. Her throat was dry, her voice a rasp.

"Negative, sir. An unknown quantity."

Lisa stood up and moved to the visor viewport. "I want visuals as soon as possible, and get Exedore and Breetai up here on the double!"

"Well?" Lisa said from the command chair, tapping her foot impatiently. Klaxons squawked as the ship went on alert. She had not forgotten about the EVA craft, but there were new priorities now.

Exedore turned to look at her. "These are not Tirolian ships, Admiral, I can assure you."

Breetai and Rick were with him, all three men grouped behind the tech seated at the threat board. "Enhancements coming in now, Lisa," Rick said without turning around.

The computer drew several clamlike shapes on the screen, pinpointing hot areas.

Breetai straightened up and grunted; all eyes on the bridge swung to fix on him. "Invid troop carriers," he announced angrily.

"Invid? But what—"

"Could they have formed some sort of alliance with the Masters?" Lisa thought to ask.

"That is very unlikely, Admiral," Exedore answered her.

Rick spoke to Lang, who was still on-screen. "We've got company, Doctor."

"The ship must be protected."

"Sir!" a tech shouted. "I'm showing multiple paint throughout the field!"

Rick and the others saw that the clam-ships had opened,

yawned, spilling forth an enormous number of small strike mecha. Pincer Ships, Breetai called them.

"I want the Skull scrambled."

"Ghost Squadron is already out, sir," Blake reported from his duty station.

"What!"

The threat board showed two clusters of blips moving toward each other. Rick slapped his hand down on the Situation Room com stud, demanding to know who ordered the Veritechs out.

"General Edwards," came the reply.

"Edwards!" Rick seethed.

Blake tapped in a rapid sequence of requests. "Sir. Ghost Squadron reports they're moving in to engage."

Cabell was puzzled. It was not Zor's ship after all, but some sort of facsimile. Worse, the Invid had sent its small fleet of troop carriers against it, and their Pincer Ships were already engaging mecha from the Zentraedi ship out near Fantoma's rings. Initially, Cabell wanted to convince himself that the Zentraedi had for some reason returned in Micronized form; but he now dismissed this as wishful thinking. It was more likely that the starship had been taken by force, and he was willing to guess just who these new invaders were. Presently, data from one of the network computers confirmed his guess.

He had pulled up trans-signals received by the Masters shortly after the destruction of Reno's fleet and the capture of the factory satellite. Among the debris that littered a vast area of space some eighty light-years out from Tirol were mecha almost identical to those the would-be Zentraedi had sent against the Invid. These invaders, then, would have to be the "Micronians" whose world the Masters had gone off to conquer, the same humanoids who had been the recipients of Zor's fortress, and with it the Protoculture matrix.

And while Invid and Terrans formed up to annihilate each other, a small ship was leaving Tirolspace unobserved. Watching the ship's trail disappear on his monitor screen, Cabell smiled to himself. It was the Elders, fooled like himself perhaps, into believing that the Zentraedi had returned. *For their skins!* Cabell laughed to himself.

So Tirol was suddenly Masterless. Cabell considered the battle raging out by the giant's ring-plane, and wondered aloud if Tirol was about to change hands yet again.

In the Royal Hall Invid headquarters, Obsim was thinking along similar lines. These starship troopers were not Zentraedi, but some life-form similar in makeup and physiology to the population of Tirol or Praxis. And yet they were not Tirolians either. By monitoring the transmissions the invaders were radioing to their mecha pilots, the brain had discovered that the language was not that of the Masters.

"Sample and analyze," Obsim commanded.

It was a primitive, strictly vocal tongue; and the computer easily mastered it in a matter of minutes, along with the simple combat code the invaders were using.

Obsim studied the communications sphere with interest. The battle was not going well for his Pincer units; whatever the invaders lacked in the way of intellect and sophistication, they possessed powerful weapons and mecha more maneuverable than any Obsim had ever seen. A world of such beings would not have been conquered as readily as Spheris, Praxis, and Karbarra had. But firepower wasn't war's only prerequisite; there had to be a guiding intelligence. And of this the invaders were in short supply.

"Computer," said Obsim. "Send the mecha commanders

new dictates in their own code. Order them to pursue our troops no matter what."

The starship itself was hiding inside Fantoma's ring-plane; but if it could be lured out for only a moment, the troop carriers might have a clear shot at it.

Obsim turned to face the brain. "Computer. Locate the starship's drives and relay relevant data to troopship commanders." He contemplated this strategy for a moment, hands deep within the sleeves of his robe. "And prepare to advise the Regent of our situation."

The tac net was a symphony of voices, shrill and panicked, punctuated by bursts of sibilant static and the short-lived sound of muffled roars.

"Talk to me, Ghost Leader," a pilot said.

"Contact, fifty right, medium range . . ."

"Roger, got 'im."

"Ghost Three, Ghost Three, bogie inbound, heading zero-seven-niner . . ."

"Ghost Six, you've got half-a-dozen on your tail. Go to Battloid, Moonlighter!"

"Can't get—"

" . . ."

Rick cursed and went on the com net. "Ghost Leader, do you require backup? Repeat, do you require backup? Over."

"Sir," the pilot replied an instant later. "We're holding our own out here, but it's a world of shi— er, pain, sir!"

"Can you ascertain enemy's weapons systems? Over."

Static erased the pilot's first few words. ". . . and some sort of plasma cannons, sir. It's like they're throwing . . . -ing energy *Frisbees* or something! But the mecha are slow—ugly as sin, but slow."

Rick raised his eyes to the ceiling of the bridge. *I should be out there with them!* Breetai and Exedore had returned to their stations elsewhere in the ship; and by all rights Rick should have been back in the Tactical Information Center already, but everything was happening so damned fast he didn't dare risk pulling himself away from a screen even for a minute. Lisa had ordered the SDF-3 to Fantoma's brightside, where it was holding now.

"Has anyone located General Edwards yet?" Rick shouted into a mike.

"He's on his way up to the Sit Room, sir," someone replied.

Rick shook his head, feeling a rage mount within him. Lisa turned to watch him. "Admiral, you better get going. We can manage up here."

Rick looked over at her, his lips tight, and nodded.

"Sirs, enemy are in retreat."

Rick watched the board. "Thank God—"

"Ghost is in pursuit."

Rick blanched.

"Contact them! Who ordered pursuit—Edwards?!"

Blake busied himself at the console. "Negative, sir. We, we don't know who gave the order, sir."

"Direct the Skull to go—*now!*" Rick raced from the bridge.

Lisa regarded Fantoma's ring-plane and remembered a similar situation in Saturn's rings. "Activate ECM," she ordered a moment later. "We're bringing the ship up. And, dammit, send someone out to rescue that EVA craft!"

Jonathan Wolff left the SDF-3 launch bay right behind the last of Max Sterling's Skull Squadron fighters. He was in a Logan Veritech, a reconfigurable mecha that would one day become the mainstay of the Southern Cross's Tactical Armored Space Corps. The Logan was often jokingly referred to as a "rowboat with wings" because of the bow-shaped design of its radome and the mecha's overall squatness. But if it was somewhat less orthodox-looking than the Alpha, the Logan was certainly as mean and maneuverable—and much more versatile—than the VT. In addition, the mecha's upscaled cockpit could seat two, three in a pinch.

Scanners had indicated there were two people aboard the hapless EVA craft that had been caught up in the SDF-3's fold. And they were alive, though more than likely unconscious or worse. There had been no response to the fortress's attempts to communicate with the craft.

Empowering the fortress's shields had made use of the tractor somewhat iffy, so Wolff had volunteered for the assignment, itching to get out there anyway, even if it meant on a rescue op. Now suddenly in the midst of it, he wasn't so sure. Local space was lit up with spherical orange bursts and crisscrossed with blue laserfire and plasma discs of blinding light. Zentraedi Battlepods were one thing, but the ships the VTs found themselves up against looked like they had walked out of some ancient horror movie, and it was easy to believe that the crablike mecha actually *were* the XTs themselves. But Breetai and Exedore had said otherwise in their prelaunch briefings; inside each ship was a being that could prove swift and deadly in combat.

And that was indeed the case, as evidenced by the slow-mo dogfights in progress all around Wolff. Skull's VTs were battling their way through the remnants of the Invid's original strike force in an effort to catch up with the Ghost Squadron, who'd been ordered off in pursuit of the main group. Wolff watched amazed as Battloids and Pincer Ships swapped volleys, blew one another to fiery bits, and sometimes wrestled hand-to-pincers, battering each other with depleted cannons. Wolff watched Captain Miriya Sterling's red Veritech engage and destroy three Invid ships with perfectly placed Hammerhead missiles. Max, too, seemed to be having a field day; but the numbers were tipped in the enemy's favor, and Wolff wondered how long Skull would be able to hold out.

He was closing fast on the EVA craft now, and thought he could discern movement in the rear seat of the cockpit. But as the Logan drew nearer, he could see that both pilots were either unconscious or dead. Reconfiguring now, he imaged the Battloid to take hold of the small ship and propel it back toward Fantoma's brightside and the SDF-3. But just then he received a command over the net to steer clear, and a moment later the fortress emerged from the ring-plane and loomed into view. Inexplicably, the Skull Squadron was falling away toward Fantoma's opaline surface, leaving the ship open to frontal assaults by the Pincer units, but in a moment those ships were a mere memory, disintegrated in a cone of fire spewed from the SDF-3's main gun.

Harsh static crackled through Wolff's helmet pickups as he turned his face from the brilliance of the blast. But when he looked again, two clam-shaped transports had materialized out of nowhere in the fortress's wake.

Reflexively, Wolff went on the com net to shout a warning to the bridge. Secondary batteries commenced firing while the fortress struggled to bring itself around, but by then it was too late. Wolff saw the SDF-3 sustain half-a-dozen solid hits, before return fire sanitized the field.

A score of lifeless men and women lay sprawled across the floor of the fortress's engineering hold. Damage-control crews were rushing about, slipping in puddles of blood and cooling fluids, trying to bring dozens of electrical fires under control. A portion of the ruptured hull had already self-sealed, but other areas ruined beyond repair had to be evacuated and closed off by pocket bulkheads.

Lang and Exedore ran through smoke and chaos toward the fold-generator chamber, arriving in time to see one of the ruptured mechanisms vanish into thin air.

Lang tried to shout something to his team members above the roar of exhaust fans, but everyone had been nearly deafened by the initial blasts.

Just then a second explosion threw Lang and Exedore to the floor, as some sort of black, wraithlike images formed from smoke and fire and took shape in the hold, only to disappear from view an instant later.

Lang's nostrils stung from the smoke of insulation fires and molten metals. He got to his feet and raced back into the chamber, throwing switches and crossovers at each station. By the time Exedore got to him, Lang was a quivering, burned, and bloodied mess.

"They knew j-just where to h-hit us," he stammered, pupilless irises aflame. "We're stranded, we're *stranded* here!"

CHAPTER
EIGHT

I'm of the opinion that in this instance Lang (with regard to Janice) was emulating the Masters—or more accurately perhaps, serving Protoculture's darker side. Zand, and anyone else who conspired to control, was serving this purpose as well. Protoculture's bright side had yet to reveal itself, for what had it wrought so far but conquest, war, and death? Indeed, it could be argued that Protoculture's only bright moment came at the end, when the Regis wed herself to it and was transformed.

Mingtao, *Protoculture: Journey Beyond Mecha*

OBSIM WAS PENSIVE AS HE REGARDED THE COMMUN-icator sphere; four troop carriers and countless Pincer Ships had been lost, but he had achieved a good portion of his purpose: the invaders' starship was crippled if not destroyed. It had come into full view now from Fantoma's brightside, and was holding in orbit near the giant's outer rings. ECM had foiled Obsim's attempt to reach the Regent, but a messenger ship had since been dispatched and reinforcements were assured.

But what now? the Invid scientist asked himself. Surely the outsiders recognized that Tirol would soon be entering Fantoma's shadow. Would they then move the ship into orbit, risk some sort of landing perhaps?

Well, no matter, Obsim decided. The command ships would be there to greet them.

On the fortress, meanwhile, a mood of apprehension prevailed while the RDF licked its wounds and counted the dead. Unprovoked attack was one of many scenarios the crew had prepared for, but the Invid hadn't been seriously considered. Lang, for one, had thought that the Zentraedi had all but eliminated the race; and while he remembered the image of an Invid ship included in Zor's SDF-1 "greetings message," neither Exedore nor Breetai had been forthcoming in supplying him with any additional information. Moreover, the arrival of the "Visitor," and the subsequent Robotech War, had left the Earth Forces with the mistaken notion that *humankind* dominated the galaxy. Although the Zentraedi were giant, biogenetic clones, they were still in some way understandable and *acceptable*. But not so this new enemy wave. There had of course been prelaunch briefings that addressed the alien issue, but the Zentraedi's descriptions of the Invid, the Karbarrans, the Spherisians, might as well have been campfire ghost stories or horror-movie tribute—*War With the Newts*! So as rumors began to spread through the ship, everyone was left asking themselves why the mission had once seemed a sensible idea. And Lang had yet to tell everyone the really bad news.

In an effort to curtail some of the loose talk, Rick called for a immediate debriefing following the return of Ghost and Skull squadrons. Everything would have to be kept secret until all the facts were known.

He was pacing back and forth in one of the ship's conference rooms now, while the general staff and squadron commanders seated themselves at the U-shaped arrangement of tables. Livid, he turned to Edwards first, calling for an explanation of the man's motives in superseding command's orders regarding engagement. Edwards listened attentively while Rick laid it out, allowing a pregnant silence to fill the room before responding.

"The SDF-3 was under attack, Admiral. It was simply a matter of protecting the ship."

Rick narrowed his eyes. "And suppose those ships had come in peace, General—what then?"

Edwards snorted, in no mood to be censured. "They didn't come in peace."

"You risked the lives of your men. We had no idea what we were going to face out there."

Edwards looked across the table to the Ghost Squadron commanders. "My men did their job. The enemy was destroyed."

Rick made a gesture of annoyance, and turned to the VT pilots. "I want to know why your teams gave pursuit. Who gave those orders?"

Max stood up. "Admiral, we received orders to pursue."

"With the proper authentication codes?"

"Affirmative, sir," half-a-dozen voices murmured at once.

Rick knew that he could do little more than demand a report, because Edwards could only be censured by the Council itself. Where Rick and Lisa would ordinarily have had complete run of the ship, the dictates of the Plenipotentiary Council had forced them to share their command with Edwards and other representatives of the Army of the Southern Cross apparat. This was the arrangement that had been made to satisfy the demands of Field Marshal Anatole Leonard's burgeoning power base in Monument City. Edwards's presence, in fact, was an accommodation of sorts, an appeasement undertaken to keep the RDF and Southern Cross from further rivalries—the Expeditionary Mission's peace treaty with itself. The last thing anyone wanted was to have the SDF-3 return to a factioned and feudal Earth. Moreover, Edwards was the xenophobic voice of those Council members (Senators Longchamps and Stinson, chiefly, the old guard of the UEDC) who still felt that Captain Gloval and the SDF-1 command had been too soft with the Zentraedi during the Robotech war—granting asylum for the enemy's Micronized spies and suing for peace with Commander Breetai. And as long as Edwards continued to enjoy support with the Council, Rick's hands were tied. It had been like this between generals and governments throughout history, he reminded himself, and it remained one of the key factors that contributed to his growing discontent.

Rick glanced at Edwards. "I want full reports on my desk by fourteen-hundred hours. Is that understood?"

Again, Rick received eager nods, and talk switched to the issue of secrecy. Rick was listening to descriptions of the mecha the VTs had confronted, when a lieutenant jg entered with a personal message. It was from Lang: the EVA craft had been taken aboard and its passengers moved to sick bay.

Rick went pale as he read the names.

It was a terrible dream: there she was on stage all set to perform, and the lyrics just wouldn't come. And it seemed the hall was in space with moons and planets visible in the darkness where an audience should have been sitting. Then Rick was, what?—God! he was coming down the aisle with Lisa on his arm . . .

Minmei's eyes focused on Rick's face as she came around. She was in bed and he was leaning over her with a concerned look. She gave him a weak smile and hooked her arms around his neck.

"Oh, Rick, what a dream I had—"

"Minmei, are you all right?" He had unfastened her embrace and was holding her hands.

"Well, yeah," she began. "Except for that . . ." Then it hit her like a brilliant flash.

Rick saw the shock of recognition in her eyes and tried to calm her. "You're aboard the SDF-3. You're safe, now, and the doctors say you'll be fine."

"Where's Janice, Rick!"

"She's right next door." Rick motioned. "And she's okay. Dr. Lang is with her."

Minmei buried her face in her hands and cried, Rick's hand caressing her back. "Why did you do it, Minmei?" he asked after a moment.

She looked up and wiped the tears away. "Rick, I just couldn't let everyone leave. You're all so important to me. Do you understand?"

"You could have been killed, do you understand that?"

She nodded. "Thank you for saving me."

Rick cleared his throat. "Well, actually you'll have to thank Colonel Wolff for that. But listen, you better get some rest now. There's a lot I have to tell you, but it'll keep."

"Thank you, Rick."

"Go to sleep now," he said, standing up and tucking her in.

She was out even before Rick left the room, so she didn't see the orderly who entered, or the astonished look Rick gave the bearded man. It was a look of recognition, but one tinged with enough disbelief to render the first impression false. But as the orderly studied Minmei's sleeping form, he recalled how *he* had once protected her from giants and worse.

*   *   *

In the room adjacent to Minmei's, Dr. Lang was staring into Janice's blue eyes. Her skills had certainly saved Minmei's life, but why had Janice listened to Minmei in the first place? Their little stunt had destroyed all the plans he had taken such pains to set in motion; and coming as it did on the heels of the damage done to the fold generators and what that meant for the Expeditionary mission, it was almost more than he could bear.

"Janice," he said evenly. "Retinal scan."

Janice's eyes took on an inner glow as she returned Lang's all but forehead-to-forehead stare. But in a moment the glow was gone; her eyes and face were lifeless, and her skin seemed to lose color and tautness.

"Yes, Dr. Lang. Your request."

"I want you to replay the events prior to SDF-3's departure, Janice. I want to understand the logic of your decisions. Is that clear?"

"Yes, Dr. Lang," Janice repeated in the same dull monotone.

Lang laughed to himself as he listened. He had foreseen the *possibility* of such an occurrence, but to be faced with the reality of that now . . . That part of the android that was its artificial intelligence had actually developed an attachment, a *fondness* for Lynn-Minmei! The specter of this had been raised and discussed repeatedly by the Tokyo Center's team, but in the end Lang had rejected the safeguards they had urged him to install, and suddenly he was face-to-face with the results of that uninformed decision.

The android had taken more than a decade of intensive work; but when Janice took her first steps, all those hours and all that secrecy seemed justified. It was shortly after the destruction of New Macross that Lang had begun to think about teaming the android with Lynn-Minmei, and the singer had easily been convinced of just how important such a partnership might prove to Earth's safety. But defensive harmonies aside, Lang had chosen Minmei because of her undenied access to political sanctuaries Lang himself could not enter, the Southern Cross apparat especially. So Lang was understandably thrilled to learn that Senator Moran had taken an interest in Janice, the young sensation some people were calling his niece, some his mistress. But what good was his spy to him now, stranded as she was along with the rest of them light-years from Earth.

Lang uttered a resigned sigh as he reached behind Janice's neck to remove the dermal plug concealed by her fall of thick hair. The plug covered an access port Lang could tap for high-speed information transference. He had the portable transfer tube prepared, and was ready to jack in. But just then Rick Hunter came through the door.

Undetected, Lang dropped the tube behind the bed and voiced a hushed command to Janice. Hunter was staring at him when he turned from his patient.

"Uh, sorry, Doc, guess I should've knocked first," Rick said uneasily.

"Nonsense," Lang told him, getting to his feet.

Rick looked back and forth between Lang and Janice; he didn't know Minmei's partner all that well, but he was aware of the scuttlebutt that linked her to Lang. Janice was offering him a pale smile now.

"How are you feeling?" he asked.

"Homesick," Janice said. "And less than shipshape."

"Well I don't know what we're going to do about your homesickness, but I'm sure some rest will help the way you're feeling."

"That's good advice," Lang seconded. He switched off the lights as he and Rick left the room.

"She's . . . sweet," Rick said, uncomfortable with the silence the two men fell into.

At the elevator, Jonathan Wolff stepped out from the car, managing a salute despite the two bouquets of flowers he carried. "Thought I'd try and cheer up our new passengers," he said by way of explanation.

Rick and Lang traded knowing looks.

"Guess every SDF's meant to carry civilians, huh, Admiral."

"Does seem that way, Colonel," Rick said. "Minmei's in room eleven," he added, motioning with his chin.

Wolff moved off down the hall, and Rick and Lang entered the elevator. "I think our dapper young colonel has more than good cheer on his mind," Lang opined.

Rick felt his jaw. "Doesn't he have a wife and coupla kids back home?"

"Ask him."

Rich shrugged. "It's none of my business."

A second debriefing was held later that afternoon. In addition to those who had attended the earlier session were Commander Vince Grant, Brigadier General Reinhardt, Wolff, Lang, Breetai, and Exedore, along with various squadron and company commanders. Photo images and schematics filled the room's numerous screens this time; the crew was still on standby alert, and the ship would shortly reposition itself for an orbital shift.

Lang at last revealed that two of the spacefold generators had been destroyed during the assault. He explained that a fold might still be possible, but there was no guarantee the fortress would emerge in Earthspace, and anything short of that was unacceptable. The twelve-member Plenipotentiary Council had voted to withhold this information from the crew. But it was therefore imperative that the Masters be contacted as soon as possible.

"The Invid presence might prove a blessing in disguise

for us," Lang continued. "Because if the Masters are indeed being held captive on Tirol, the Expeditionary mission could well be their salvation."

Lang called up an image of the Fantoma system on the main screen. Like Uranus, the planet had been tipped on its side eons ago. It had an extensive ring system held in check by shepherd satellites, and numerous moons of varied size and surface and atmosphere. Tirol was the third moon, somewhat smaller than Earth, and the only one with an hospitable atmosphere. It was, however, a somewhat desolate world, barren, with much of its topography muted by volcanic flows. Just why the Masters had chosen to remain there with half the galaxy at their disposal was a question Lang had recently added to his long list. In a matter of days the moon would enter Fantoma's shadow, which could complicate things considerably.

"Surface scans and intensity traces have given us the picture of an almost deserted world," Lang added as a closeup of Tirol came up on the screen, "except for this one city located close to Tirol's equator. I have proposed to the general staff that we begin here."

Rick stood up to address the table. "There's evidence the city's seen a lot of nasty action lately, so we've got to assume the Invid have a strong presence down there. I think our best move is to drop the GMU to recon this entire sector and ascertain the Invid's strengths. The SDF will be holding at a Lagrange point, so you'll have all the backup you need in case we've underestimated their defensive capabilities. Any questions so far?"

The men shook their heads and grumbled nos.

"Has everyone received the new authentication codes?" Rick directed to Grant and Wolff.

"We have, sir."

"I've asked Lord Exedore—" Lang started to say when Breetai interrupted him.

"Exedore and I have decided that my troops should accompany Commander Grant's ground forces."

Rick regarded the Zentraedi with an appraising look. "You're not required to become involved with this, Commander Breetai. You're not under our command . . ."

"That has nothing to do with it, Admiral. You seem to forget that I have walked this world."

Rick smiled. "I haven't forgotten . . . Grant, Wolff, do you have any problems with this?"

Vince shook his head and extended his hand to Breetai. "Welcome aboard, Commander."

"Well, that's settled," Lang said, getting to his feet again. "I have one thing to add. It concerns the Invid ships." Perspective schematics of a Pincer Ship took shape while he spoke. "Their central weakness seems to be this scanner that looks like some sort of mouth. So direct your shots there if it comes to that."

"And I hope it won't," Rick interjected. "It's possible that our initial confrontation was a misunderstanding, and I don't want us going down there like liberators. This is still a *diplomatic* mission, and you are only to engage if provoked." Rick shot Edwards a look. "Is that understood?"

"Affirmative," Wolff and Grant answered him.

"All right, then," Rick said after a moment. "Good luck." *And I wish I could be down there with you*, he said to himself.

The dropship hangar bay was the scene of mounting tension, tempers, and liveliness when the word came down to scramble. Men and women ran for gear and ordnance while the massive GMU rumbled aboard the ship that would take it planetside. Jack Baker was among the crowd,

Wolverine assault rifle in hand as he lined up with his teammates for a last-minute briefing. Like the rest of them he had missed yesterday's EV action, but stories had spread among the ranks of an engagement with some new breed of XTs, who flew ships that resembled giant one-eyed land crabs. And now the GMU had been chosen to spearhead a ground assault on the Robotech Masters' homeworld. Jack would still have preferred piloting an Alpha Fighter with the Skull, but under the circumstances this op was probably the next best thing to that.

He looked down the long line of mecha pilots waiting to board the dropship and spied Karen Penn just as she was donning her helmet, blond hair like fire in the red illumination of the hangar.

"Karen!" he yelled, waving and hoping to get her attention above the sound of alert klaxons and high-volume commands. He was tempted to give it one last try, but her helmet was on now and he knew he wouldn't be heard. He did, however, lean out of line to watch her rush up the ramp.

At the same time, he peripherally caught sight of a captain taking angry strides toward him. Hurriedly, Jack tucked his chin in, steeled himself, and muttered a prayer that the line would get moving.

"Just what the hell was that all about, Ensign!" the captain was yelling into his face an instant later. "You think this is some kind of goddamned *picnic*, bright boy! You've got time to wave to your friends like you're off on some cruise! Well, let me tell you something, you deluded piece of space trash: it's no picnic and it's no cruise! You got that, you worthless little sublife protein! Because if I see you stepping out of line again, you're going to be sucking vacuum before we even hit!"

Jack could feel the woman's spittle raining against his

face, but told himself it was just a cooling sea spray wash-
ing over the bow. The captain continued ranting for a while
longer, then gave him a powerful shove as the line suddenly jerked into motion.

Oh well, he reminded himself, *the worst she could do
was chew him out, which didn't amount to much considering there were things down there waiting to kill him.*

In another part of the hangar, Minmei was saying thank-
you to Jonathan Wolff. A personal note from Admiral
Hunter had gotten her past security, and now she and Wolff
were standing by the broad and flattened armored bow of
the dropship. Several Micronized Zentraedi were gaping at
the singer from a respectable distance, but Breetai soon
appeared on the scene and hurried them to the ship with
some harsh grunts and curses.

"I just had to thank you before you left," Minmei was
saying. "Janice wanted me to tell you the same. You saved
our lives, Colonel." She vaguely remembered him from the
wedding; but then she had met so many men during those
few hours . . . Still, there was something about Wolff that
caught her attention now. Maybe it was the mustache,
Minmei told herself, the man's swashbuckler's good looks
and tall, broad-shouldered figure. She wished she had chosen some other outfit to wear. The RDF uniform just
wasn't cut right for her shape.

Wolff didn't seem to mind it, however. "Actually the
honor could have gone to anyone," he said, showing a
roguish grin. "But I was lucky enough to volunteer."

Minmei liked that. "Janice and I were just trying to get a
better look at the fortress, and all of a sudden . . . well, you
know."

Wolff's eyebrows arched. "Really? That's strange, because I had your flight recorder checked, and it seems you two actually flew directly into the vortex of the ship's spacefold flash point."

Minmei's face reddened. "Well, whatever happened, I'm glad about it now."

"Me, too," Wolff said, holding her gaze.

Suddenly Minmei went up on tiptoes and kissed him lightly on the corner of the mouth. "Be careful down there, Colonel."

Wolff reached for her hand and kissed it. "Can I see you when I get back?"

"I'd like that, Colonel—"

"Jonathan."

"Jonathan." She smiled. "Take care, Jonathan."

Wolff turned and was gone.

"That little fool," Lisa said after Rick told her about Minmei. They were alone in a small lounge not far from the bridge. "What was she trying to do, get herself killed?"

"You have to see it from her side," Rick argued. "She felt like everyone she cared about was leaving her."

Lisa regarded him suspiciously. "No, I don't *have* to see things from her side. But I'm sure you were understanding with her, weren't you? Did she cry on your shoulder, Rick?"

"Well, what was I supposed to do? You know I'd send her back if we could."

"I wonder," Lisa said, folding her arms.

Rick made a conciliatory gesture. "Whoa . . . Look, I don't like where this one's going. She's here and there's nothing we can do about it, okay?"

Lisa looked at him for a moment, then stepped in to lean her head on his shoulder. They hadn't had a chance to say two words to each other for more than twenty-four hours, and their comfortable bed was beginning to feel miles away. They were both exhausted and still a little stunned by the events that had transpired since they'd *gone off to work*!

"Is it the honeymoon you hoped for?" Rick asked, holding her.

She let out her breath in a rush. "It's the nightmare I wished we'd never have to live through." She pulled back to gaze at him. "We came here to sue for peace. And now . . ."

"Maybe that doesn't exist anymore," Rick said, turning to the viewport as Tirol loomed into view.

In the nave of Tiresia's transformed Royal Hall, Obsim listened patiently to the computer's announcement. A flash of synaptic sparks danced across the brain section's fissured surface, strobing orange light down at the scientist and a group of soldiers who were gathered nearby. For the past several periods the starship had been trying to communicate with Tirol, but Obsim had elected to remain silent. If indeed they had come in "peace," why were they equipped with such a mighty arsenal of weapons? More confusing still, their ship and mecha were Protoculture-driven, a fact that linked them beyond a shadow of a doubt to the Masters' empire.

And now they were sending one of their transport dropships to the moon's surface, just as he had guessed they would.

"Tell the Command ships to prepare," Obsim instructed his lieutenant. "And have your units stand by for a strike-ship assault."

"And the Inorganics, Obsim?" the lieutenant asked. "Will the brain reactivate them now?"

Obsim came as close to smiling as his physiognomy allowed. "In due time, Enforcer, in due time."

CHAPTER
NINE

I suppose I should have been surprised that it didn't happen a lot sooner. Rick never believed that he was cut out to command, and I can remember him already trying to talk himself into resigning his commission when work first began on the SDF-3. I wanted to get to the bottom of it, but he didn't want my help. Basically he didn't want to hear his fears contradicted. So I was left to puzzle it out like a mystery, and I was convinced that both Roy Fokker's death and Rick's continuing "little brother" attitude had a lot to do with his behavior.

Lisa Hayes, *Recollections*

IT WAS AN HISTORIC MOMENT: THE DROPSHIP'S ARRIVAL on Tirol marked the first occasion humankind had set foot on a world outside the Solar system. But it was business as usual, and that business was *war*.

The GMU rumbled down out of the dropship's portside ramp onto the moon's barren surface, and within minutes Wolff was shouting "Go! Go! Go!" into the Hovertank cockpit mike as his Pack left the mobile base. Their landing zone was at the foot of a towering black ridge of impossibly steep crags; but soon the Pack was moving across a barren stretch of seemingly irradiated terrain. The massive GMU dwindled behind the twenty-unit squadron as they formed up on Wolff's lead and sped toward Tirol's principal city—Tiresia, according to Breetai. It was late afternoon on Tirol.

The Hovertanks were ground-effect vehicles; reconfigurable assemblages of heavy-gauge armor in angular flattened shapes and acute edges, with rounded downsloping deflection prows. In standard mode, they rode on a cushion of self-generated lift, but mechamorphosed, they were either Battloid or guardian—squat, two-legged waddling mecha the size of a house, with a single, top-mounted particle-projection cannon.

Wolff called up the GMU on the comlink for a situation report, and Vince Grant's handsome brown face surfaced on the mecha's cockpit commo screen. A defensive perimeter had been established around the base, and so far there was no sign of activity, enemy or otherwise. "You've got an open channel home," Vince told him. "We want to know everything you're seeing out there."

Wolff rogered and signed off. There were no maps of Tiresia, but bird's-eye scans from the SDF-3 scopes had furnished the Pack with a fairly complete overview. The city was laid out like a spoked wheel, the hub of which appeared to be an enormous Cheops-like pyramid. Eight streets lined with secondary buildings radiated out from the center at regular intervals, from magnetic north right around the compass. Nothing came close to rivaling the pyramid in size; in fact, most of the structures were the rough equivalent of three stories or less, a mere fraction of the central temple.

Exedore had described Tiresia's architecture as approximating Earth's Greco-Roman styles, with some ultratech innovations that were Tirol's alone. This is precisely what Wolff found as his Pack entered the city; although hardly a learned man, Wolff had seen enough pictures and renderings of Earth's ancient world to corroborate the Zentraedi ambassador's claims.

"Um, fluted columns, entablatures, peaked pediments," he radioed back to the GMU. "Arches, vaults . . . buildings that look like the Parthenon, or that thing in Rome—the Colosseum. But I'm not talking about marble or anything like that. Everything seems to be faced with some non-porous alloy or ceramic—even the streets and courtyards."

But this was only half the story, the facade, as it were. Because elsewhere were rectilinear and curved structures of modernistic design, often surrounded by curious anten-nalike towers and assemblages of huge clear conduits.

And much of it had been reduced to smoldering rubble.

"I'm splitting the squadron," Wolff updated a few min-utes later. Straight ahead was the central pyramid, still a good distance off but as massive as a small mountain in Tirol's fading light. He switched over to the mecha's tacti-cal net. "A team will follow me up the middle. Winston, Barisky, take your team over to the next avenue and paral-lel us. But stay on-line with me. One block at a time, and easy does it."

"Roger, Wolff Leader," Winston returned.

"Switching over to IR scanners and moving out."

There was still no sign of the Invid, or anything else for that matter, but Wolff was experiencing an itchy feeling he had come to rely on, a combat sense he had developed during the Malcontent Uprisings, hunting down renegade Zentraedi in the jungled Southlands. He checked his cock-pit displays and boosted the intensity of the forward scan-ners. At the end of the broad street where it met the hub were a pair of stacked free-floating columns with some sort of polished sphere separating them. He was close enough to the pyramid base now to make out a stairway that ascended one face; the pillared shrine at the summit was no longer visible.

Just then Winston's voice cracked over the net, loud in Wolff's ears.

"We've got movement, Wolff Leader! Multiple signals all over the place!"

"What's your position, Boomer?" Winston gave the readings in a rush. "Can you identify signatures? Boomer, do you copy?"

"Nothing we've seen," the B-team leader said over a burst of angry static. "Bigger than either ship those flyboys registered. *Much* bigger."

"On our way," Wolff was saying when something thirty feet tall suddenly broke through a domed building off to his left. It was an inky black bipedal ship, with cloven feet and arms like armored pincers. The head, equally armored, was helmet-shaped but elongated in the rear, and sandwiched between two nasty-looking shoulder cannons. Wolff watched spellbound as orange priming charges formed at the tips of the cigar-shaped weapons. An instant later two radiant beams converged on one of the Hovertanks and blew it to smithereens.

Wolff gave the order to return fire as four more enemy ships emerged from the buildings and a fifth surfaced in front of him, *right out of the damned street!*

The Hovertanks reconfigured to Gladiator mode and singled off against the Invid, the streets a battle zone all at once, filled with heavy metal thunder and blinding flashes of explosive light. Wolff saw another of his number go down. On the tac net, Wilson reported that his team was faring no better.

"Go to Battloid mode. Pull back and regroup," he ordered. Then he tried to raise the GMU.

* * *

In the GMU's command center, Vince Grant received word of the recon group's situation: four, possibly five, Hovertanks were down and Wolff was calling for reinforcements or extraction. His Pack had been chased to the outskirts of the city, where they were dug in near the remains of what the colonel described as "a kind of Roman basilica."

"Tell him to hold on, help's on the way," Grant told the radio man. Then he swung around to the command center's tactical board. At about the time Wolff's Pack had been ambushed, Invid troops had begun a move against the mobile base itself. Deafening volleys were rolling in from the line, echoing in the sawtooth ridge at the GMU's back. Night had fallen, but it was as if someone had forgotten to inform Tirol's skies.

"Ground forces are sustaining heavy casualties in all perimeter zones," a com tech updated without having to be asked. "The enemy are employing mecha that fit yesterday's profiles, along with teams of one-pilot strike ships."

The commander studied a computer schematic as it turned and upended itself on the screen. Vince tried to make some sense of the thing. *A deadly kazoo*, he thought, *with forward guns like withered arms and an undercarriage cluster of propulsion globes*. Whatever they were, they were decimating the forward lines. He had already lost count of the wounded and dead.

"Wolff on the horn, Commander," a tech said. "He's requesting backup."

"Get his present location," Vince told the woman.

The tech bent to her task, but got no response. She tapped her phones and repeated Wolff's call sign and code into the net.

Vince leaned over the console and hit the com stud. "Go ahead, Colonel. We're reading you. Colonel."

"God, I don't believe it!" Wolff said at last.

"Colonel," Vince said more loudly. "Respond."

"They're . . . they're going after my men, pulling them out of the tanks . . ."

Several command-center techs turned to watch Vince at the com station. "Who is, Colonel?"

The net was silent for a moment; then Wolff added, "Cats, Commander. Some kind of goddamned *cats*!"

Grant lifted an ashen face to the room. "Notify Breetai that his Battlepod team has a green light."

"Bah," Cabell muttered, switching off the remote sensor's audio signal. "Our Bioroids were a better match for the Invid than these Earthers. It's a mystery how they defeated our Zentraedi."

Rem kept his eyes on the monitor screen while the old man swiveled to busy himself with other matters. Almost two dozen Human mecha had entered the city, but there was scarcely half that number now. They had successfully turned the tide against the Command ships that had surprised them, but Invid reinforcements had since appeared on the scene. The remains of countless Hellcats littered the streets the Humans had chosen for their last stand.

"But Cabell, isn't there some way we can help them?"

The scientist showed him his palms. "With what, my boy? We are effectively trapped down here." He motioned to the Pollinators who were peacefully huddled in a corner. "Would you drive these ferocious creatures against them?"

Rem made an impatient gesture. "We can tell the Humans about the Royal Hall."

"Break radio silence?" Cabell asked. "And draw the Invid right to us?"

"Would you rather the Invid inherit our world?"

Cabell stroked his beard and regarded the youth. "How like him you are . . ."

Rem beetled his brows. "Who?"

"Uh, why, your father of course," Cabell said, turning away. "He, too, would have thought nothing of such a sacrifice. But listen, my boy, how can we be certain these Humans are any better than the Invid? After all, we know the Invid's capabilities. But the Humans' ways are unknown to us."

Rem gestured to the screen. "Perhaps this will change your mind, Cabell."

Skeptical, Cabell faced the screen: a score of Battlepods had arrived to back up the Terran tanks.

"Zentraedi mecha," the brain announced. "*Regult* and *Glaug*."

"Yes," Obsim said, registering some surprise. "So there is a connection between these invaders and our old foes." He looked back and forth from the communicator sphere to the living computer. "Perhaps we are in some jeopardy, after all. Computer: evaluate and advise."

"Extrapolating from previously displayed battle tactics . . ." the brain began. "Defeat for our ground forces in seven point four periods unless reinforcements arrive from Optera. Substantial damage to aliens' mecha and casualties in excess of six hundred; but not enough to threaten their victory."

"Advise, then."

A bundle of raw energy ascended the floating organ's stem and diffused in the region of the midbrain. "Conserve our strength. Take the battle to the invaders' base. Sacrifice the troopers to keep the invaders from the city. And await the arrival of reinforcements."

Obsim mulled it over. "Is there more?"

"Yes," the brain added a moment later. "Protect the brain at all costs."

"Headless ostriches" was the term VT pilots had given Battlepods during the Robotech War. Bipedal, with re-verse-articulated legs and a laser-bristled spherical command module, the pods had been designed for full-size warriors. There was just enough room for a single, fully expendable pilot, and little in the way of cockpit padding or defensive shielding. But Lang's teams had reworked the mecha, so that they could now be operated by two Micronized pilots with plenty of room to spare. RDF mechamorphs were trained in pod operation, but there existed an unspoken taboo that kept Humans to their own mecha and Zentraedi to theirs.

But there were no such lines drawn when Breetai's team leaped in to lend the Wolff Pack a much-needed assist. Battlepods and Hovertanks fought side-by-side hammering away at the Invid Command ships. Pulsed-laser fire and conventional armor-piercing projectiles split Tirol's night. An entire quadrant of the city burned while the battle raged, and friend and foe added their own fire and smoke to the already superheated air.

The Hellcat Inorganics had abandoned the scene, as though frightened off by the pods, and now the Command ships were suddenly turning tail.

Wolff sat in the mecha's seat, convulsively triggering the Hovertank's weapon as the enemy ships disengaged and began to lift off. The colonnade of a building collapsed behind him, sending gobs of molten metal airborne. He raised the GMU on the net to update his situation.

"We're being overrun," a panicked voice informed him in response. "Commander Grant says to pick yourselves up and get back here ASAP!"

Wolff ordered his few remaining tankers to reconfigure, and addressed Breetai. "We're moving out. The base is ass deep in pincers."

"At your command, Colonel," the Zentraedi responded, pleased to be taking orders once again, to have an imperative to follow.

Every bed and table in the GMU's med-surg unit was filled, and still the wounded kept coming. The mess hall was a triage area and battle dressing station now, and Jack Baker had found himself in the midst of it, pulled there from supply to lend a hand. All around him men and women were stretched out on the floor and tabletops in postures of distress and agony. A young woman with third-degree burns across half her body flailed her arms against the restraints a medic was attempting to fasten, while a nurse struggled to get an IV drip running. Elsewhere a man drugged beyond pain stared almost fascinated at the bloody stump that had been a leg less than an hour before. Some of the wounded groaned and called on God and relatives for help; but Jack saw others expire with no more than a whimper, or a final curse.

Jean Grant, the front of her surgical gown red-brown from blood and antiseptic washes, was moving from table to table checking wounds and shouting orders to her staff.

"Move it, soldier!" Jack heard someone behind him yell. He felt the edge of a stretcher smack against his hip, and turned as two women medics rushed past him bearing a lieutenant he recognized to surgery.

A warrant officer called to him next, waving him over to a bloodied expanse of wall, three bodies slumped lifelessly against it. "These men are dead," the officer announced, getting to his feet and wiping his hands on his trousers. "Get them out of here, and get yourself back up here on the double." The officer looked around. "You!" he said, finding another aide in the crowds. "Get over here and give this man a hand!"

Jack bent down to regard the dead, unsure where to begin.

"You take his arms," a female voice said over his shoulder. Karen Penn was beside him when he turned. She gave him a wan smile and wiped a damp strand of hair from her face with the back of her hand, leaving a smear of someone's blood on her cheek.

"I want to get out there," Jack grunted as he lifted the body. "Some paybacks are in order."

"Maybe that's what this guy said," Karen bit out. "Let's just do our job and forget the heroics."

"We'll see."

When they had eased the body down onto the floor in the next room, Karen said, "If I see your sorry face show up in here, I'm going to remind you of that remark."

"You do that," Jack told her, breathing hard.

The SDF-3 was still at its orbital holding point above Tirol. The general staff was kept informed of the situation below by continuous updates from the GMU. One such report was coming into the fortress now, and T. R. Edwards left the TIC's balcony rail to listen more closely. A tech loyal to the cause was making adjustments for reception, and punching decoding commands into the console.

"It's from Grant, sir," the tech reported, seeing Edwards peering over his shoulder. "The situation has deteriorated and is growing untenable."

Edwards glanced around the balcony area. Hunter and Reinhardt had gone off to meet with Lang and some of the council members. "Speak plainly, Lieutenant," he said, narrowing his eye.

"They're getting their butts kicked, sir. Grant is requesting air support from the ship."

Edwards straightened up and felt the stubble on his chin. "How do we know this isn't some enemy trick, Lieutenant? Did the GMU use the proper authentication codes?"

"Affirmative, sir."

Edwards was silent while the planetside transmission repeated itself. "But then they broke our code once already."

The tech risked a grin. "I think I understand, sir."

"You'll go far," Edwards told him, leaning in to dial the gain knob down to zero.

At the same time Edwards was gloating over having eliminated Vince Grant from his life, Minmei was fantasizing about how to get Jonathan Wolff into hers. It was the flower arrangement the colonel had had delivered to her cabinspace that kicked off the fantasy; obviously he had called in the order before he left, perhaps right after they said good-bye in the dropship hangar. She was toying with the flowers now, lost in a daydream, while Janice studied her from across the room.

"Keep fooling with those things and they're going to wilt before they have a chance to bloom," Janice said from the couch.

Minmei showed Janice a startled look, then gave the arrangement one last turn before she stepped back to regard it.

"You're thinking about catching that bridal bouquet, aren't you?"

Minmei smiled. "How could you tell?"

"Because sometimes I can read you like a screen," Janice sighed. She patted the cushion next to her. "Come over here, you."

Minmei fixed two drinks and sat down, kicking off her shoes and curling her legs beneath her. Janice sipped at her glass and said, "Now tell your partner all about it."

"Do you believe in omens?"

"Omens?" Janice shook her head. "First I'd have to believe that the future has already been written, and that's simply not the case. Reality is shaped and reshaped by our words and deeds."

"I'm not asking you *philosophically*, Janice."

Janice took another sip and glanced at the flowers. "You think destiny has thrown you and Jonathan Wolff together."

Minmei nodded. "Don't you?"

"No. Not any more than I think destiny brought you and me together. We have a tendency to highlight moments we wish to think preordained."

"I promised myself I'd never get involved with a military man," Minmei continued, as though she hadn't heard Janice. "Not after Rick. And now here I am worrying about Jonathan, just the way I used to worry about Rick." She met Janice's eye. "I don't want to lose him, Janice."

"Worrying doesn't change anything, Lynn."

"Then what does it matter if I worry? Maybe I just didn't worry *enough* about Rick."

" 'They also serve . . .' " Janice mused.

"Huh?"

"Just something I heard once." She took Minmei's hand. "Go ahead and worry. We all have our appointed tasks."

"I'm sick of having to listen to everyone," Rick complained bitterly, sitting down on the edge of the bed. He and Lisa had taken advantage of a short break to rendezvous in their quarters. "The council has decided we should recall the GMU and leave Tirolspace. Suddenly they're all convinced this bloodshed has been a misunderstanding. They want to remove our 'threatening presence'—those are their words—and try to open lines of communication. Station a small unarmed party out here or something..." Rick exhaled forcibly. "War of the worlds...Even Lang has reversed himself. Ever since his teams started picking apart those Invid mecha we salvaged. All at once he's fascinated with these butchers."

Lisa rested her hand on his shoulder. "Don't do this to yourself, Rick."

He looked up at her, eyes flashing. "Yeah, well, I'm tired of being the one who has to walk around with his guts tied up."

"Rick, nobody's asking you—"

"My place is with the VTs. I just wasn't cut out for command."

Lisa kneeled down to show him the anger in her own eyes. "Maybe you weren't, if you're going to talk like that. But first tell me who we should have in command. And tell me what good you think you can do in combat?"

"Are you saying I'm rusty?"

Lisa's eyes went wide. "Stand down, mister, I'm not saying that at all. I'm asking you what good it's going to do to add another *combatant* to the field, when what we need is some enlightened decision making." She relaxed her gaze. "You're not thinking clearly, Rick. You need some rest, we're all frazzled."

"Maybe you're right," he allowed.

The door tone sounded just then, and Max entered.

"Rick, Lisa. Sorry to barge in."

"It's all right, Max," Rick said, getting to his feet. "What's up?"

Max hesitated for a moment. "Rick, why are we ignoring the GMU's requests for backup?"

Rick stared at Max blankly. "What are you talking about?"

"They've been sustaining heavy losses down there."

"Why wasn't I informed of this? Who's in the Situation Room now?"

"Edwards."

Rick cursed under his breath. He gave Lisa a brief kiss and grabbed hold of Max's arm, tugging him from the room.

The two men burst into the Tactical Information Center a few minutes later. Rick glanced once at Edwards and demanded an update from a tech.

"Colonel Wolff and Commander Breetai have pulled out of Tiresia with scarcely half their command, sir. Latest reports shows them in sector November Romeo—"

"Admiral!" a second tech shouted from further along the threat-board console. "Priority transmission from the GMU."

"Go ahead," Rick told him.

The tech listened for a moment, then swiveled to face Rick again. "They say they're receiving transmissions. From Tirol, sir—from somewhere in the city. The message is in Zentraedi, sir."

"Have they identified themselves?"

"Negative, sir, other than to say they are Tiresians, and that they have important intelligence for our forces."

"A trick," Edwards spat. "An Invid trick. They've been sending in false messages all morning."

Rick regarded him a moment, then turned to Max. "Scramble the Skull, Commander. Get down there and lend support."

"Aye, aye, sir." Max saluted, leaving the room in a rush.

"Tell Commander Grant to continue monitoring transmission," Rick instructed the tech. "I want them to patch us in so we can hear it for ourselves." Rick slapped his hand down on a mike switch. "Notify Exedore and Dr. Lang to meet me in the briefing room. I'm on my way now!"

Rick ran for the door, already considering the decisions he would have to make.

Cabell's age was incalculable, as had been the case with Exedore, Breetai, and several other Zentraedis who'd permitted Zand's team to study them. But whereas the warrior clones had been "birthed" full-size and ageless, Cabell had enjoyed an actual childhood, adolescence, and adulthood. His decision to undergo the Protoculture treatments that fixed his age was a conscious one. It has yet to be demonstrated how DNA and Protoculture combine to allow this miracle to occur. Like the Micronization process, it remains a complete mystery.

Louie Nichols, *BeeZee: The Galaxy Before Zor*

"**M**Y NAME IS CABELL. I AM TIROLIAN SCIEN-tist. Our people are being held prisoner by the Invid in structures throughout the city. The Invid ships and Inorganics are receiving their orders from a computer that has been placed in Tiresia's Royal Hall. To defeat them, you must destroy the computer. And you must do this quickly. The Invid are many and merciless. Reinforcements will arrive if you do not take immediate action. My life is now forfeit; but I place the future of this world in your hands. Act swiftly, Humans, and be equally as merciless. For there is much more at stake than this tiny moon."

Cabell repeated the message twice more, then shut down the com device and turned to Rem. "Well, that does it, my boy. We have compromised our location."

Rem answered him in a determined voice. "But we may have saved Tirol, Cabell."

The old man began to look around the room, his face a mixture of rapture and longing. He ran his long fingers over the console. "Such a waste . . . What wonders we had at our disposal, what miracles we could have worked in the Quadrant."

Rem raised his eyes to the ceiling, as a sound like distant thunder shook the lab. This was followed by the sibilant burst of faraway energy beams. "It's too late for dreams, Cabell."

"I fear you're right. Their search has commenced."

Rem reactivated the communicator and gestured to the console audio pickups. "Repeat your message. We have nothing more to lose."

"The transmission is being repeated," the Invid brain informed Obsim.

"Pinpoint the source, computer."

A wiggling current coursed over folds of computer cortex. "Below this very chamber. There are vaults and corridors, a mazelike complex."

Obsim swung to an Enforcer lieutenant. "I want the Inorganics to flush them out. Tell your troops to stand by."

The soldier saluted and left the nave for an adjacent room where several Invid were watching an armored Shock Trooper bring its annihilation discs to bear on a stretch of ceramiclike floor. Already a wide wound several yards deep and as many wide had been opened.

"Continue," the Enforcer's synthesized voice commanded. "Locate and destroy."

*   *   *

"What does he mean by 'Inorganics'?" Rick wanted to know.

Lang leaned back from the briefing-room table and steepled his fingers. "I think he must be referring to the fiendish drones Colonel Wolff faced in the city. Certainly the ships we salvaged are anything but *inorganic*."

Lang tried to keep the excitement from his voice, but he was sure Rick and the others caught it. He had passed the better part of twenty-four hours in the laboratory dissecting those ships and the remains of one of the alien pilots. And what he'd uncovered about the Invid had been enough to send him into a veritable delirium. Thinking back even now to those hours of experimentation and discovery was like some wild roller-coaster ride. The very shape and form of those beings! As though they existed outside any *rules* of evolution. And the incredible similarity their brain patterns had to the emanations of Protoculture itself! The green nutrient the pilots bathed in inside their crab-ships, the myriad mysteries of the ships' propulsion, communication, and weapons systems, the integrity of pilot and ship that rendered Robotechnology's advances primitive and childlike by comparison... It had all sent him running— literally *running*!—to the Council to sue for a course other than the warlike one they had embarked on...

"Dr. Lang," Rick was saying. "I asked you if this message will be enough to change the Council's mind about leaving Tirolspace."

Lang started to reply, but Exedore's late entry interrupted him. The Zentraedi ambassador apologized and seated himself at the table between Lang and General Edwards, who was plainly disturbed by Exedore's arrival. Rick had the transmission replayed for Exedore's benefit and waited for his evaluation.

Exedore was silent for a long moment. "I . . . hardly

know what to say," he began. Rick had never seen the Zentraedi so, well, *moved*.

"Cabell," Exedore uttered. "He was a contemporary of Zor, a *mentor*, I think you would say. And to me, as well. He . . . he *made* me."

Lang and Rick exchanged astonished looks while they listened to Exedore's explanation. This Cabell had apparently been instrumental in the creation of the first biogenetically engineered clones. "Then this message is on the level, Exedore?"

"No one would use the name Cabell to evil purpose, Admiral. Of this much I am certain."

"Bullshit," barked Edwards. "This is another Invid trick. They're trying to lure us to this . . . 'Royal Hall.' Why? Because they have some sort of weapon there. They're playing with us."

"What about it?" Rick asked the table.

One of Lang's techs spoke to that. "Scanners indicate the source of the transmission is subterranean—perhaps beneath the very structure we've identified as the Royal Hall. Colonel Wolff described it as . . ." the tech checked his notes, "'a flat-topped pyramid as big as a small mountain, crowned with some kind of columned shrine.' We've picked up intense energy readings emanating from the structure."

"A weapon," Edwards interjected.

Rick tried to puzzle it out. "Suppose it is legit. Would Cabell knowingly call a strike down on his own head, Exedore?"

"Without question, if Tirol could be saved by his actions."

"Then the Robotech Masters may still be alive. Is it enough to convince the Council, Doctor, yes or no?"

"I think they'll listen to reason. But if we can possibly achieve these ends without destroying—"

"Raise the GMU," Rick instructed one of his aides. "Inform Commander Sterling that I want a recon flyby of that pyramid. I don't want anybody trying anything stupid. Tell Grant to keep the GMU dug in and wait for my word to move in."

"And Cabell?" said Exedore.

"Yes," Lang seconded. "Surely a rescue team—"

"I'm sorry, Doctor," Rick broke in. "You, too, Exedore. But I want to know what we're dealing with before we send anyone in."

Edwards snorted. "We'll say some kind words over his grave," he said loud enough for Exedore to hear.

In the tradition of that apocryphal cavalry who were always arriving in the nick of time, the Skull Squadron tore into Tirol's skies from the shuttles that had transported them to the edge of the envelope, and fell like wrathful birds of prey on the enemy's Pincer Ships and Shock Troopers. Cheers from Hovertankers and mecha commanders filled the tac and com nets as the Guardian-mode VTs dove in for missile releases and strafing runs.

Captain Miriya Parino Sterling led her team of red fighters against a group of blue-giant Command ships that were going gun-to-gun with Breetai's Zentraedi cadre. The smoking remains of Battlepods and strike ships littered a barren, now cratered expanse of high plateau where the Invid had successfully breached the GMU's forward defense lines. Miriya's Alphas hit the massive twin-cannoned mecha where they lived, chattering undercarriage guns stitching molten welts across cockpit shields and torso armor, and red-tipped heat-seekers finding the ships' vulnerable sensor mouths. Explosions geysered fountains of white-hot alloy into the waning light as ship after ship fell, leaking viscous green fluids into the dry ground. Renewed, the Battlepods leaped to regain their lost ground, trading energy salvos with the larger ships, their orange and blue bolts cutting swaths of angry ionization through the moon's thin atmosphere.

Elsewhere, Max's blue team backed up the Wolff Pack's devastated Hovertank ranks, reconfigured to Battloid mode for close-in combat, while overhead, solitary Veritechs went to guns with the less maneuverable Shock Troopers. Ships boostered and fell, executing rolls and reversals as they engaged.

Even the GMU's main gun was speaking now, adding its own thunderous punctuation to the battle's murderous dialogue. A second and third wave of mecha burst from the base's forward ramps—Mac II cannons, Excalibers, and drum-armed Spartans—but the Invid would neither fall back nor surrender.

It was all or nothing, Max realized as he bracketed two of the alien ships in his sights. Missiles tore from the Battloid's shoulder racks and found their mark; the ships came apart in a dumbbell-shaped cloud of flame and thick smoke. In the end, once the RDF's debris was carted from the field, it would look like a slaughter had taken place; but in the meantime men and women continued to die.

Max ordered the Battloid into a giant-stride run, pulled back on the selector lever, and imaged the VT through to fighter mode. He went ballistic, instructing his wingmen to follow suit, and was about to rejoin Miriya when Vince Grant's face appeared on one of the cockpit commo screens.

"You've got new orders, Commander, straight from the top."

"Uh, roger, Home. Shoot."

"Your team's to recon the Triangle. Just a flyby with a minimum of sound-and-light. Do you copy, Skull One?"

"Can do, Home. Waiting for your directions."

"We're punching them in now," Vince said.

Max's onboard computer came alive, stammering vectors and coordinates across the display screen.

"And Max," Vince added. "Be sure to keep in touch."

Evening's shadow was once again moving across Tirol's face; a crescent of Fantoma loomed huge in the southern skies, its ring-plane a shaft of evanescent color. The battle was over—for the time being, forever, no one could be sure, any more than they could be sure who had won. If it went by the numbers, then the RDF had been victorious; but there was no known way of conveying that to the five hundred who had died that day.

Jack had been returned to his outfit and was out at the perimeter now, finally out on Tirol's surface, where he felt he should have been all along. There was a good deal of activity going on around him—mecha tows and transports and APCs barreling by, VTs flying recon sweeps—but he still wasn't content. He had been assigned to take part in a mine-emplacement op, which meant little more than observing while Gladiators planted and armed AM-2 Watchdogs across the field. (These anti-mecha mines of high-velocity plastique had been developed by one Dr. R. Burke—who was also responsible for the Wolverine assault rifles—and came complete with an Identification Friend or Foe targeting microchip housing a library of enemy ground signatures, even those recently cooked up by the GMU's computers to indicate Invid Scouts and Shock Troopers.) So instead of giving the Gladiator his undivided attention, Jack had slipped away to eavesdrop on a conversation that was in progress at one of the forward

command posts. Jack understood that the enemy had been
soundly defeated, but things were a still bit sketchy with
regard to follow-up plans. He sensed that something important was up, and in a short time he had the astounding
details.

A message had been received from Tirol's occupied
city—sent by some sort of rebel group, from the sound of
it—giving the location of the Invid's central command.
The Skull had been ordered to recon the site, but nothing
was in the works to save the rebels themselves, who were
apparently holed up in the very same neighborhood. Having seen a crude map of Tiresia, Jack knew the place
would be easy enough to suss out. And if a small team—
even *one man*—could infiltrate, the rebels would be as
good as free. All it took was the *right* man.

But chief among the things Jack *didn't* know was that
his actions over the past hour had been observed at rather
close range by Karen Penn. And she stuck with Jack now
as he began to angle his way behind the command post and
into the forward supply area. He waited until the sentries
were preoccupied, then moved in and grabbed hold of a
Wolverine and an energy-pack bandolier. Karen drew her
hand weapon and decided it was time to confront him.

Taken by surprise, Jack swung around with his hands
raised, prepared to assume the position. But realizing it
was Karen, he simply shook his head and shouldered past
her. Karen armed the handgun, which came to life with a
short-lived but unmistakable priming tone. It stopped Jack
in his tracks.

"Now, you want to talk to me, Jack, or the unit commander?"

"Look," he said, turning around carefully, "there's
something I've got to do." He explained what he knew

about the communiqué and the rebel group, and how a small group could get in and out unnoticed.

Karen listened without comment, then laughed shortly and deactivated her weapon. "You're certifiable, you know that?"

Jack made a face. "I'm going in alone, Karen."

"Oh no you're not," she said, grabbing a Wolverine from the rack. "'Cause I'm coming with you."

Jack showed her a grin. "I know where there's a coupla Hovercycles."

Karen pulled the bandolier's straps taut. "Lead on, hero," she told him.

Obsim peered into the trench the enforcers had opened in the floor of the Royal Hall. Fifty feet down they had broken through the roof of a narrow corridor, a stretch of the mazelike subterranean works the brain had discerned.

"The Inorganics will locate the Tiresians within the period," the brain informed Obsim when he reentered the Hall's central nave.

"I am pleased," Obsim said, trying on a regal tone.

"There are other concerns . . ."

"Prioritize."

"A group of airborne mecha are closing on our position."

Obsim glanced at the communicator sphere, where a holo-image of six blue Veritechs was taking shape.

"Advise, computer."

"Protect the brain. Activate the shield."

Obsim tried to calculate the resultant energy drain. "You are so instructed," he said after a moment of reflection.

Bubbles formed, percolating in the brain's tank.

"It is done."

*   *   *

Max had his team complete two high-altitude passes over the city before dropping in for a closer look. Schematics of Skull's topographical scans had revealed that Tiresia's Royal Hall was an enormous structure indeed, a truncated pyramid almost a thousand feet tall capped by a classical Roman-like shrine. It dominated the city, which was itself a kind of circular mandala set into Tirol's bleak surface. Scanners had also picked up dusk activity in the city's street; but whatever was moving around down there was smaller than the Invid ships the Skull had thus far gone up against.

"All right, let's stay alert," Max said over the net as the team followed him down. "Keep an eye on each other. Blue Velvet, you've got the number-one spot."

"Roger, Skull Leader, I'm on my way," the mechamorph responded.

Max watched him peel away from the group, roll over, and drop in for the run. They were all closing on the Hall, scarcely five hundred feet above it, when a translucent envelope of scintillating energy suddenly mushroomed up in front of them. The envelope expanded to encompass the entire Hall, and with it, Blue Velvet's lone Veritech. The rest of the team broke hard and climbed.

"It's a force field of some kind," Max said. "Blue Velvet, get yourself out of there!"

"No can do, Skull One, my systems are down! Reconfiguring and going for touchdown . . ."

Max was heading back toward the Hall again, and could see the Guardian-mode VT falling. But all at once there were three bizarre shapes on the shrine steps—headless, demonic-looking bipedal mecha, with dangling arms and orifice-dimpled weapon spheres.

"You've got company, Blue Velvet!" Max shouted the pilot's call sign twice more, but got no response. The

Alpha was preparing to land when the creatures opened fire and blew it off course.

Max watched helplessly as the Veritech grazed the edge of the pyramid and exploded, raining fiery debris down the Hall's steep side.

"Hit them!" Max ordered.

Missiles dropped from the Veritechs' undercarriage pylons and ripped in twisting tracks toward the Inorganics, only to detonate harmlessly against the Hall's repellent dome. But the enemy could fire through the shield and did, catching a second VT before Max could order the team away. He was trying to decide what to do next, when one of his wingmen came on the net. "Skull Leader, I'm picking up two friendly blips down below."

Max listened for the coordinates, tipped his Alpha, and leaned over to take a look. "You sure they're friendly?"

"Affirmative. The IFF says they're Hovercycles. They're approaching the Hall."

Hovercycles, now what the . . . Max said to himself. "All right," he said, "let's go down and see what's cooking."

"Wha-*hoo!*" Jack shouted, throttling the Hovercycle down a slope of arid ground and onto one of Tiresia's central spokes. "Life in the fast lane!"

"Idiot," Karen muttered to herself, goosing the handbar grip in an attempt to catch up with him. "He's going to get us both killed."

The cycles were face-effect vehicles, with conventional grips, right-angled bars rising up and back from a single shaft, and a front Hover-foot that resembled an old-fashioned carpet sweeper. The seat and backrest was a sweeping, padded affair, and although the cycles were built for one, the rear storage deck could accommodate a second rider if need be. They were fast, silent, and maneuverable, but essentially weaponless.

"What are you trying to prove?" Karen said, coming up alongside Jack's cycle. "Is this a rescue op or a joyride?"

Jack glanced over at her and began to lay out his philosophy about how self-confidence was what mattered most; but instead of listening she was just looking at him wide-eyed, and the next thing he knew, she had her handgun raised and aimed in his general direction—

"Duck!" she yelled, firing off two quick bursts that nearly parted Jack's carrot-colored hair.

"Jeez!" he said, when they'd brought the cycles to a halt. "Whaddaya think—"

"Take a look at that."

Jack twisted around in the seat and spied the Inorganic Karen's shot had neatly holed. Still on its feet and slumped against a wall, the thing reminded him of a character from an old cartoon. "Tasmanian devil," Jack recalled, snapping his finger, as the Crann slid to the smooth street.

"Is it alive?" Karen asked, looking around warily.

"Not any more."

"But what is it?"

"I don't know," Jack said, bringing the Wolverine off his shoulder, "but there's three more of them coming our way."

Karen reholstered her sidearm and followed Jack's lead. Suddenly, half-a-dozen blue energy bolts were zipping past her, impacting against a wall and sending up a shower of white-hot gunk. A blast of superheated air washed over her, stinging her eyes and nose while she brought the assault rifle to bear on the drones.

Jack was already firing; his rounds had managed to connect with one of the Inorganics, and Karen watched as the thing flashed out and crumbled, as though hollow. An instant later the other two went down, breaking open like ceramic figurines.

"Let's get out of here!" Jack yelled, as bolts began to rain down on them from surrounding rooftops.

Karen kept up with him, piloting the cycle one-handed while she loosed an arc of rear fire, dropping two more Cranns with well-placed sensor shots. "What now?" she said, her voice raspy from the heat, smoke, and all the shouting.

Jack motioned up the street, toward a small mountain of a structure. "Straight ahead. That's the Hall. The message originated from somewhere underground. I figure there's gotta be a way down."

"You figure," Karen said in disbelief. "I'm for turning back."

"Uh-uh. But I am for *turning*!"

Karen looked up: ten or more Inorganics were blocking the street. Their weapons were raised.

Perplexed, Cabell regarded the weapon Rem had given him; he fumbled with the rifle's selector lever. "Like this?"

"No, no, Cabell," Rem said, close to losing his patience. "Like this," he demonstrated, activating his own weapon.

Cabel mimicked Rem's movements. "Ah, I see . . . and you hold it like, er, you put your right hand, um, let's see, you—"

"Give me that thing!" Rem snapped, snatching the rifle from the old man's hands. Cabell was offering him a imbecilic shrug. "You'll probably vaporize your own foot."

"I wouldn't doubt it for a moment," Cabell agreed. "I'm sorry, I've never had any talent for the fine art of combat. Why, back when the Masters were first—"

"Save it, Cabell. Are we going or not?"

Cabell took one long last look around the room. Still-functioning remotes had permitted them to view the Humans' recon attempt, and later, their failure to breach the barrier shield the Invid computer had deployed. But with Inorganics closing on the subterranean lab now, there was no time for further monitoring of the situation. Cabell had insisted that they not be caught in the lab. The Pollinators would be his gift to the Invid; with them and some seedling Flowers, perhaps they could refoliate ravaged Optera, end this incessant killing . . .

"Well, what have we here?" Cabell said suddenly.

Rem came back into the lab, cursing, and found the scientist pointing to one of the screens. Here were two Humans just outside the force field, a male and a female, straddling strange-looking Hovercrafts.

"Could they be searching for us, Rem?"

"Don't flatter yourself," Rem answered him, tugging Cabell into the corridor. They could hear the Inorganics nearby, blasting through corridor walls and breaking into rooms.

"But they *could* be looking for us."

Rem continued to drag Cabell down the corridor. "Fine, fine . . ."

Cabell reached for one of Rem's weapons. "Then let's just go out and meet them."

CHAPTER
ELEVEN

Finally all the principal players had been introduced to one another: Masters and Invid, Zentraedi and Humans, Humans and Invid, Humans and Masters. Surely this was Protoculture's doing; but what would make the contest especially bizarre was the fact that not one of those players had all the puzzle pieces. It was a mad, mad, mad, mad world.

Dr. Emil Lang, *The New Testament*

THE REGENT WAS RELAXING IN HIS BATH WHEN OBSIM'S message finally reached him. The sunken tub in his private chambers was as large as a backyard swimming pool, surrounded by ornate fixtures the Regis had detested. *You have too many things,* she used to scream. *Things!*—when the very goal had always been to move away from such material trappings. Her goal, at any rate. *Freedom from this base condition* . . . her words to describe their world after the affair with Zor. After Optera, an Eden if ever there was one, had been defoliated by the Masters' warrior clones, robbed of the Flower that was infinitely precious to the Invid, so *essential*. They were like starving creatures now, feeding off what nutrients had been stored up in their flesh, but hungry, ravenous for sustenance only the Flower could provide.

The Regent sighed as he climbed from the tub, regarding the sterile green bath fluids with a mixture of sorrow and disdain. To be sure, the bath had been drawn from Flowers and fruits, but a mutated variety from Peryton that had to pass for the real thing, for absent, too, were the Pollinators, those shaggy little beasts critical to the Flowers' reproductive cycle. As a result, the Regent no longer bathed to empower himself, but simply to sustain a memory of brighter times.

Brighter times indeed, he told himself as a servant moved in to drape a robe over him. *You have taken a wrong turn*, the Regis had warned him. *A turn toward de-evolution and evil purpose*. She was already in Tiresioid form then, desperate in her attempts to emulate Zor's race. She had begged the Regent to join her in that novel guise, but he would hear nothing of it. His queen, his *wife*, had been defiled, his world contaminated, and still she would ask for such a thing. When his very heart was burning with a rage never before known to him. Was it any wonder then that he had chosen his own course? The goal—the goal, my *dear*—is conquest and consumption; and *things*— warriors and weapons and battle mecha—are pivotal to that end.

To hell with her if she couldn't understand his purpose!

And yet . . . and yet how lonely this place seemed without her. Surrounded by nothing but servants and soldiers now, he could almost miss the arguments of those final days. The passion. She had fled with half her brood to carry on with her mad experiments in transmutation, her quest for the perfect physical vehicle to inhabit while she completed her Great Work, a form more suitable for her wisdom and dreams, more supportive than his embrace.

"Curse her!" he seethed, taking quick steps toward the antechamber.

A messenger genuflected as he entered, lowering its head and bringing an arm to its breast. The Regent's Hell-cats were restless, pacing the room, sniffing and snarling. He put them at ease with a motion of his hand and bade the messenger rise and state its purpose.

The messenger handed over a voice-imprint and withdrew. The Regent activated the device and listened, running it through again and again until satisfied that he had memorized Obsim's every word, every nuance.

Tirol under attack—by what Obsim had initially believed were Micronized Zentraedi, but were now thought to be a coalition of Zentraedi and some unknown Tiresioid race. A race of beings with Protoculture-driven starships and mecha! *This* was the astonishing thing Protoculture could only be derived from the Flowers, and the potent Flowers were indigenous to Optera, and Optera *only*. Look what had become of those seedlings Zor himself had tried to implant on Karbarra, Spheris, and the rest.

"What could it mean?" the Regent asked himself. An undiscovered world, perhaps, rich in the Flower that was life itself, ripe and waiting to be plucked.

He summoned the messenger to return. "Make haste to inform Obsim that reinforcements are on their way." He turned to his lieutenants next, his stingraylike hood puffed up, betraying his agitation.

"The Regis is not to learn about these matters. This new world will be our . . . our *present* to her."

But only if she agrees to listen to reason, he kept to himself. *Only if she accepts the path of conquest!*

The Regent's huge hand closed on the voice device, splintering it to bits.

* * *

Jack and Karen stood transfixed at the edge of the Royal Hall's shimmering shield, unsure of what they were up against. They had given the enemy drones the slip for the moment, but there was no time to dally.

"I say we try to go in," Jack was saying.

Karen gazed into the field's evil translucency. "And I say you ought to have your head examined."

"Maybe if I just touch—"

Jack reached his hand out before she could stop him, and in a flash was flat on his back unconscious.

Karen screamed and ran to him, kneeling by his side, wondering if there was anything she could do, her hands fluttering helplessly. "You stupid idiot!"

Jack came to and looked up at her stupidly, then shrieked as the pain caught up to him. His left hand flew to his right wrist, clutching it as though aware of the torment above. Karen pried Jack's fingers loose and pulled his hand to her. It was blanker than a newborn's, void of prints and lines. She told him to lie still, ran to the idling Hovercycle, and returned with a first-aid kit. She hit him with a pre-loaded syringe of painkiller and waited till it took effect.

Jack's face was still beaded with sweat a moment later, but the drugs had done their job; he offered her a weak smile and forced his breath out in a rush. "Now, what was that you were saying?"

"About you needing to have your head examined? Forget it." She showed him his effaced palm. "You're going to need a whole new personality."

"No big deal," Jack muttered. "The old one was about used up anyway."

"I'm glad you said it." Karen laughed, helping him to his feet. "Now let's get back to base."

They started for the cycles, only to swing back around to the sound of metal-shod feet. Five Hellcats came tearing around the corner, for some reason slithering to a halt instead of leaping. The drones fanned out and began to stalk the two Humans as they backed themselves slowly toward one of the Hovercycles. Karen had her blaster drawn.

"Nice kitties," Jack said in a calming voice. "On three we leap for the cycle," he told Karen out of the corner of his mouth.

"But—"

"Don't worry, I can drive. You keep those things away from us."

Karen thumbed the handgun's selector to full auto. "Ready when you are,"

"One, two . . . three!" he yelled, and they both bolted. Two of the Hellcats jumped at the same time; Karen blasted them out of the air, pieces raining down on the Hovercycle as Jack toed it into gear and took off.

A third Hellcat tried to keep pace with them, but Karen holed that one, too, right through the thing's flashing eyes. She had one arm around Jack's waist, loosing rear fire as he threw the cycle into a turn and raced down a side street.

"Where to?" she yelled.

"Left!" he answered, just as two more 'Cats leaped to the streets from the peak of a pediment.

Karen twisted on the cargo seat and laid down an arc that seared one of the beast's legs off. But others were joining in the pursuit; she stopped counting at eleven.

"How's our fuel?" she thought to ask.

"Going fast," he said, his bad hand up by his shoulder, comically mouthing the words. "Any suggestions?"

"Yeah. Remind me to let you go it alone next time something like this comes up!"

"I've got them, Skull Leader," one of the VT team confirmed. "They're both on the same cyc now, west of the

Hall on a connecting street between two of the main spokes. 'Bout a dozen drones behind them."

"Have they spotted you, Blue Lady?"

"Uh, negative. They've got their hands full. Some rough terrain up ahead—craters, devastated buildings . . ."

"Can you exfiltrate?" Max asked her.

Blue Lady fell silent, then said, "Think I see a way."

"Coming around to cover you."

"I'm going in," the woman announced to her Beta copilot. "Breaking hard and right . . ."

"Heads up, you two!" a female voice shouted from the Hovercycle's control pad speaker.

Jack thought he was hearing things and wondered if his brush with the force field hadn't damaged more than just his hand. Karen was discharging bursts from the cargo seat, but for every drone she killed another two would appear; it was as if some controlling intelligence was directing the chase.

Jack had been forced to take some bad turns back toward the Royal Hall, and was trying to puzzle out a way through the wreckage in front of them when that disembodied voice repeated itself.

"Heads up!"

Even Karen heard it this time, so Jack knew he wasn't imagining it. "An Alpha," she said, waving her free hand in his face. He looked up and saw the VT dropping in to match the Hovercycle's pace and course.

"Looks like you two are a long way from home," the pilot said. "I'm coming in for a pickup. Acknowledge."

"Fine with us," Jack said. "Hope she's not changing her mind?" he added when the VT didn't respond.

Karen interrupted her fire to peer over Jack's shoulder. She smacked him on the shoulder. "You idiot, use the net!"

Jack winced and opened the net, acknowledging the VT.

The Alpha dropped and let loose with two missiles that took out half the Hellcat pack; then the mecha split, its Beta hindquarters lowering a stiff ladder.

"Grab it," Jack told Karen.

They were near the central plaza again in an area of the city that had seen a lot of action, skirting the rim of a huge blast crater.

Karen holstered her weapon, got into a kneeling position on the seat using Jack's shoulders for balance, and took hold of the ladder, heat from the VT blasting her face all the while.

"Come on, Jack!" she was shouting into the wind a moment later.

Jack stretched out his bad hand, thought better of it, and took his good hand from the front grip. Karen curled herself on the ladder and leaned down to help him. But all at once, two Hellcats came tearing out of an alleyway making straight for the cycle. Jack caught sight of them in time, but forgot about his injured hand as he reflexively reached for the handlebars.

Pain like liquid fire shot up his arm. Out of control, the Hovercycle veered to the right and ramped up the rim.

Jack felt himself leave the cyc's contoured seat and go airborne. In an instant's passing, he was once again questioning his sanity, because floating out in front of him he saw some kind unanchored column—two of them, actually, separated by an equally free-floating featureless sphere. Jack impacted the uppermost column at the same moment he heard the Hovercraft crash in the smoky crater below him. His hands, knees, and feet tried to find purchase, but he soon found himself sliding . . .

He hit the sphere and clung there a moment, wishing he had suction cups instead of hands, then recommenced his slow slide, flesh squealing along the thing's smooth surface.

"Whaaaaa . . ." he sent into Tirol's evening chill.

Jack's fingertips somehow managed to catch the edge of the lower column. Breathless, he hung there, nose buried in one of the flutes as the Beta circled him. And all at once his hand began to remember something . . .

He screamed and let go, recalling the hotfoot he had given a cadet back in academy days, and hit the ground with enough force to instantly numb both his legs.

On his butt now, dazed and hurting, Jack directed some choice words against himself.

Muttering, he tried to stand up.

Six pairs of glowing eyes were approaching him out of the crater's groundsmoke.

"Can you see him?" Karen asked the Beta's pilot, as she threw herself from the ladder into the mecha's passenger space.

"Not yet," the pilot answered her with a hint of anger. "I've got a biosensor reading, but there's just too much smoke down there."

Karen tried to peer out the canopy. "We've got to go back."

"Suddenly you're not suicidal."

"Hey, look," Karen said, "we just went—"

"Tell it to the judge," the pilot cut her off. "I've got one of them, Skull Leader," she said over the net. "Number two's on his own. The cyc's a memory."

Karen heard Commander Max Sterling reply, "Reconfigure and go in. But keep it simple. First sign of big stuff and I want you out of there."

"Understood, Commander. Reconfiguring . . ."

*   *   *

Jack slapped his hip holster and gulped. He was weaponless, and the cat drones had effectively cut him off from
whatever remained of the Hovercycle. Not that Jack was
even sure he could find it in all the smoke. He turned
through a three-sixty looking for some way out, and spotted the partially-ruined archway of an ancient-looking
building. He ran for it without hesitation, ignoring the
shock waves each ankle sent up his quivering legs.

Presently, he could discern broad steps in front of him, a
short flight that led to a pillared platform, and beyond that
the arch. Galloping, clanking sounds told him that the Inorganics weren't far behind.

But there was another sound in the midst of all that
eye-smarting smoke: the sound of a Beta's VTOL flares.
Jack realized that the mecha had changed modes and was
descending. Trouble was, it was putting down on the
wrong side of things. Six drones were standing between
him and rescue.

Jack decided to try and wait it out; let the VT handle the
drones, then show himself when the coast was clear. He
limped his way up the stairs and hastened toward the building.

All at once a Hellcat landed in front of him. Jack dug
his heels in and threw himself behind one of the columns
as the creature leaped. He felt the closeness of its passage,
and began to scramble around the column base, while the
Hellcat turned and leaped again. It hit the opposite side of
the pillar with a resounding crash, its clawed paws em-
bracing the base and almost tearing into Jack where he
stood. Jack jumped for the next column and the next, sla-
loming his way down the platform one step ahead of the
infuriated drone.

He reached the end of the row and tumbled down a
flight of steps. The Hellcat was above him snarling and

preparing to pounce when he rolled over. Suddenly Jack heard a weapon discharge behind him; at almost the same moment the drone came apart in a shower of fiery particles. He tucked and rolled as heat and a concussive wave battered him.

Then someone's hand touched his shoulder.

It was an old man with a bald, knob-topped head and two-foot-long snow-white beard. Jack was certain he was dreaming now.

"Good work, my boy, good work!" the man was congratulating him in Zentraedi.

Jack shook his head to clear it. Behind the man was a youth his own age, a handsome lad with tinted hair and a long cloak. He was cradling an assault rifle.

"Are you the rebels?" Jack stammered, unsure if he had chosen the correct words.

Cabell stepped back, surprised that the Human knew the old empire's *lingua franca*. "Rebels? No. But we are the ones who sent the message. I am Cabell, and this is Rem."

Rem nodded and said something in a language Jack had never heard.

Cabell nodded and pulled Jack to his feet. "Your ship," he said quickly. "We must get to your ship."

"But—"

"Hurry! There's no time!"

Cabell and Rem put Jack between them and ran in the direction of the Beta's landing zone. Jack wanted to warn them about the drones, but pain was intercepting his words. Besides, the two Tiresians seemed to be aware of the things already.

Angry flashes of orange and white brilliance were piercing the groundsmoke up ahead of them. Jack heard the characteristic chatter of the Beta's in-close weapons, and follow-up explosions he hoped accounted for the last of the enemy drones. The old man, Cabell, had most of Jack's weight now; Rem was moving out front through a hail of white-phosphoruslike debris.

Then all at once the firing was over as quickly as it had begun, and Karen's voice echoed out of an eerie silence.

She called Jack's name, but he was too weak to respond. Rem and Cabell exchanged a few unintelligible sentences, got Jack between them once again, and hastened toward the call. They were close enough to hear the Veritech's whistling hum and feel the heat its thrusters were spreading across the bottom of the crater.

The glow of running lights brought out a low moan of relief from Jack. Cabell voiced a Zentraedi greeting; Karen picked up on it after a moment and instructed them to come out with their hands raised.

She was waiting in a combat crouch by one of the VT's backswept wings when the Tiresians appeared out of the smoke. Jack thought he saw a look of astonishment on her face before Cabell and Rem set him down on the ground. She uttered something he couldn't catch and directed a question toward the Beta's open canopy.

Cabell stepped forward and addressed her.

Jack heard her nervous laugh. She had lowered the muzzle of her Wolverine, and was repeating Cabell's words for the pilot.

"You've got to be kidding."

"No, I swear it," Karen confirmed. "He said, 'Take me to your leader!'"

CHAPTER
TWELVE

Cabell impressed all of us as a kind, peace-loving man. And I knew he was one of us when he suggested that we might be able to rendezvous with the Masters in deepspace and give them what they were after (the Protoculture matrix). He'd just finished describing the horrors the Masters had spread through the Fourth Quadrant, and now he was telling us that we still had a chance to make our peace with them. Only a Human could think like that.

The Collected Journals of Admiral Rick Hunter

“I DON'T GIVE A DAMN ABOUT WHAT YOUR LITTLE escapade turned up!" Vince Grant was saying two hours later. "The only thing keeping me from throwing both of you in the brig is Admiral Hunter's request for leniency on your behalf. And when all the details of this are known, I'm sure he's going to change his mind as well. Do you read me?"

Karen and Jack swallowed hard and managed to find a collective voice. "Yes, sir; perfectly, sir."

Grant glared at them. He had his large hands pressed flat against the desk, but straightened up now and advanced to where the two former ensigns were standing at stiff attention. They had returned to the GMU scarcely an hour ago, just enough time for a pit stop at sick bay before being dragged off to Grant's office. Jack's right arm was in a sling, his head shaved and bandaged along his forehead. Karen had fared somewhat better, but perhaps because of that the commander was directing most of the flak her way.

"I would have expected as much from *him*," Grant continued, gesturing to Jack, "but I'd been led to expect better things from you, *Cadet* Penn. *Much* better things! Are you aware of the several *other* ways your self-appointed rescue mission could have turned out? Are you aware that *your* rescue endangered lives? Well?"

Karen gulped. "I am, sir. I apologize, sir."

Grant stared at her in surprise. "'Apologize,' Penn— *apologize*! That is the *least* of what you're going to be doing, believe me. Now I want to know which one of you came up with this bright idea."

"The cadet doesn't recall, sir," Karen said, eyes straight ahead.

"Really," Grant sneered, looking back and forth between Karen and Jack. "A conspiracy, huh?" Arms akimbo, he sidestepped, dark eyes flashing as he regarded Jack from his towering height. "And you, Baker . . . Born-to-be-a-hero, Baker." Grant motioned behind him. "I read you were looking for a VT assignment, is that true?"

Jack raised his eyes. "Yes, sir," he said weakly.

"You'll be lucky if you end up piloting a fanjet for the sanitation squad, mister!"

Jack blanched. "The cadet would consider it an honor to fly for the s-sanitation squad, Commander, sir."

"You bet you will, Baker."

Grant returned to his desk. "Where are the prisoners?" he asked one of his aides.

"In the holding area, sir. The shuttle and Skull Squadron are awaiting the commander's word."

Grant ran his eyes over Penn and Baker a final time. It was incredible that they had stumbled on the two Tiresians, that their joyride could possibly have resulted in just the break the RDF needed right now. But breaches of discipline couldn't be treated lightly, even when the results were more than anyone could have hoped for.

Vince knew Karen's father, and was aware of the friction between the two of them. Busted now, she would have little recourse but to follow Harry Penn's lead into research. Max, however, had appealed to Vince to go as lightly as possible; seemed that he and Rick had a special interest in Karen's fight for independence. And Baker's cause as well, although Vince couldn't quite figure it. Baker was too independent already.

"Get the prisoners aboard the shuttle, Captain. And as for these two," he said, twisting in his chair, "confine them to quarters. I don't want to see their faces. Understood?" Karen saluted, and Jack did the best he could.

"Sir!"

"Now get them out of here."

Jack followed Karen out of the office. "How about dinner in, say, six months, if we're out of this by then?" he asked under his breath.

Karen bit off a laugh. "Try me in about six years, Baker. Just maybe I'll be ready to talk to you."

Jack made a face. This wasn't supposed to be the way it worked out. But, then again, at least he had some great stories to tell over at the garbage dump.

Rick was hoping to have first crack at the prisoners, but the Council wouldn't hear of it. He had presented his case directly to Lang: the Tiresians were essentially military property; and if indeed they were the same group that had made contact with the GMU, their knowledge of the

Invid's command and control was of vital importance. "We will be certain to address that," Lang had told him. The Council had even found unexpected support from General Edwards, who still considered the Tiresian message suspect. Rick, however, had succeeded in limiting the interrogation committee to four members of the Plenipotentiary—Dr. Lang, Lord Exedore, Justine Huxley, and Niles Obstat—and four members of the RDF—himself, Lisa, Edwards, and Reinhardt.

The eight, along with security personnel, secretaries, and translators, were assembled in one of the Council's briefing chambers now, a long, narrow room with a single table and two rectangular viewports that dominated the starboard bulkhead. Tirol would be fully visible for the session, while the SDF-3's position had reduced Fantoma itself to little more than a slender background crescent. Presently, Cabell and Rem were escorted in and seated at one end of the table opposite Justine Huxley, a UEG Superior Court judge, and Niles Obstat, former senator and head of Monument City's regional legislature.

Rick heard someone gasp; when he leaned in to look to his left, he saw Lang half out of his chair.

"Is it you?" Lang was asking of the young Tiresian.

Lang's mind was racing, recalling a day more than twenty years before when he had stood in front of a data screen on the recently arrived SDF-1, and a face with elfin features and almond eyes had greeted Gloval's recon team. Then a robot with reconfigured wiring had walked into their midst, and while everyone was preoccupied, Lang had tried to activate that mainframe, had inadvertantly taken the mind-boost and altered his very life . . .

"Is it you?"

The caped Tiresian wore a puzzled look; he turned in

his seat, certain that Lang was speaking to someone behind him.

"Zor," Lang said, more shaken than Rick could ever remember seeing him. "You, you were the one . . ."

Cabell cleared his throat meaningfully and smiled, one hand on the youth's shoulder. "No." He laughed. "No, there is some resemblance—around the eyes and mouth, perhaps—but this is not Zor. Zor has been dead a long time."

Lang seemed to come to his senses. "Of course . . . I knew that."

Cabell followed Lang's gaze down the table, where it came to rest on a uncommon-looking man with dwarfish features, cropped red hair, and a thick brow ridge. The Tiresian's mouth dropped open.

"Welcome, Cabell," Exedore said evenly. "No, your eyes have not deceived you, as Dr. Lang's have."

"But, Exedore, how is this possible?" Cabell glanced from face to face, searching for other surprises, then returned to Exedore's. *The first of the Masters' biogenetically engineered clones!* The one whose very history Cabell had been forced to reshape and re-create after the Masters had turned their giant miners to warriors . . .

Little by little the story unfolded: how the SDF-1— identified by Cabell as Zor's ship—had crash-landed on Earth, and how some ten years later the Zentraedi had followed. And how a war for the repossession of that ship had commenced.

Cabell was on the edge of his seat, attentive to each added fact, and silent except when he interrupted to provide a date or refine a point.

"And the armada was actually defeated?" he said, as if in shock. "Almost five million ships . . ." Suddenly a maniacal expression surfaced. "Then, you have the *matrix*! You do have it, don't you!"

"It didn't exist," Lang answered him. "We searched—"

"No, no, no, no," Cabell ranted, shaking his head, white beard like a banner. "It does exist! You searched the fold generators, of course."

Rick, Lisa, Lang, and Exedore exchanged looks.

"Well, no," Lang said, almost apologetically. "We didn't want to tamper with the fold mechanism."

Cabell slammed his hand on the table. "It's there! It's hidden in the fold generators!"

Lang was shaking his head.

"What happened?" Cabell said, disheartened.

Exedore answered him. "The ship was destroyed by Khyron, Cabell. Its remains are buried on Earth."

Cabell grew strangely silent. He put a hand to his forehead, as though stricken. Rick recognized what he took to be a look of concern and abject terror.

"But . . . don't you see," he began. "No mere collision could destroy that device. It exists—the one source of Protoculture in the Quadrant—and the Masters have left Tirol to find it!"

"Left for *where*?" Rick demanded.

"Earth, Commander," Rem answered him.

"Oh my God," Lisa said.

Edwards and Rick looked at each other. The same names were on both men's minds, but for different reasons —Zand, Moran, Leonard. The field marshal's prelaunch warnings about Earth's vulnerability assumed a sickening immediacy. Rick suppressed a panicked scream that had seemed to lodge itself somewhere beneath his diaphragm.

"But you can overtake them," Cabell was saying. "The Masters' fortresses have superluminal drives, but there wasn't sufficient Protoculture reserves to permit a fold.

They have been gone for ten years in your reckoning. You could meet them and arrange an exchange for the device. Surely they do not want war with your world—not when there are so many worlds available to them." Cabell let his words trail off when he realized that no one was listening to him. It was at this moment that he decided to say nothing of the Elders who had left Tirolspace only a short while ago. *Let them be marooned in that cruel void*, he said to himself.

Brigadier General Reinhardt grunted sardonically. "This mission was undertaken to avoid just such a war. We came to tell the Masters that Earth didn't have what they were looking for."

"Unfortunately, we knew nothing of the situation here," Lang added. "The Invid's attack against us damaged our fold mechanism. We reasoned that by allying ourselves with Tirol . . ."

"You would have what you needed to return to your world."

"Precisely."

Cabell stared at his hands and said nothing.

"What about the message you sent our troops?" Rick cut in, anxious to return the interrogation to its central issue. "What's the situation down there?"

Briefly, Cabell explained the circumstances of the Invid's recent conquest of Tirol. He described and named the battle mecha the RDF had found itself up against: the Shock Troopers, Pincer Ships, Command ships, and the Inorganic drones—the Scrim, Crann, Odeon, and Hellcats.

"Their troops are known as Enforcers," he told the committee. "Essentially they have no independent will, save for certain evolved ones, who are thought of as 'scientists.' But the brain controls all of them."

"Brain?" said Edwards. "What is this idiocy?"

Cabell stroked his beard. "It is a computer of sorts—but much different than anything either of our races would fashion. We believe it is linked to a larger unit the Invid keep on Optera. But if you can get to the one they've placed in the Royal Hall, you will defeat them here."

"They've deployed some kind of force field," Rick said as all eyes turned to him. "So far we haven't been able to penetrate it."

"What about a surgical strike, Admiral?" Niles Obstat suggested.

Cabell stood up. "Please, Earthers, I know I have no right to ask, but our people are being held prisoner..."

Rick made a calming gesture to reassure the old man. "We're not going to do anything rash. But we do need a way in, Cabell."

"You can go in the way we came out," Rem said suddenly. "Cabell will map it out for you."

Cabell flashed his assistant an angry look. He had hoped to keep Zor's laboratory secret a while longer, but he supposed there was no hope of that now. "Of course I will," he told Rick.

Edwards was already in touch with GMU control. "Grant apparently had the same idea," Edwards reported. "He's sent the Wolff Pack in."

"The computer is invaluable," Cabell urged. "You must inform your troops that there are ways to deactivate the brain without destroying it. It could be of great use to all of us."

Edwards felt his faceplate and stared at Cabell obliquely.

It is invaluable, it controls all of them . . . It could be of great use to us. The words rolled around in his mind, settling down to a dark inner purpose.

"I want command and control," he said into the com while everyone's attention was diverted. "Get the Ghost Squadron ready for departure. I'll be down to lead them in personally."

Exedore and Lang met separately with Cabell and Rem after the committee session was dissolved. While the military faction was off deciding how best to deal with Cabell's revelations concerning the Invid brain, Lang, fully aware of the regulations he was violating, took the two Tiresians to the SDF-3's engineering section and eventually into the hold that housed the spacefold generators. On the way Cabell talked about the history of Tirol and the sociopolitical upheavals that had paved the way for the Great Transition and the emergence of Robotech Masters.

Lang and Exedore were as rapt as Cabell had been only an hour before. At last someone knowledgeable was filling in all the gaps of the saga they had tried to patch together from records found aboard the SDF-1 and the Zentraedi flagship. And how false those records were now proved to be! Even the misinformed scenarios Lang himself had worked out, the timelines he had spent countless hours assembling, the motives and explanations he had assigned.

Cabell spoke of Zor as one would of a demiurge, and in many ways Tirol's story was Zor's own—from his noble birth as a senator's only son, to his untimely death at the hands of the Regent's newly-evolved troops. Cabell told them of Zor's remarkable discovery on Optera, and of the subsequent development of Protoculture and Robotechnology; of the creation of the Zentraedi, and the growth of a new political elite; of the war that raged throughout the empire, and a renegade's attempts at rebalancing the scales . . .

Lang was given to understand that Zor, Cabell's one-time student, hadn't so much kept the secrets of Protoculture from the Masters as scattered them across the galaxy. There were still Flowers, on Optera and on many of the worlds Zor had seeded just prior to his death, but the Invid found them sterile and unusable because their Pollinators had also been taken. And while the Masters were in possession of these curious creatures, *they* no longer had the matrix that allowed for Protoculture conjuration from the Flowers. Zor had seen to it that no one could profit from his discoveries; and in the end he had driven himself half mad, convinced that he could somehow rule over all of it and parcel out to the universe the gift of everlasting life.

Exedore and Lang learned a little about Cabell, also; about how he and Zor and several other Tirolian scientists had deliberately refused to embark on the dangerous course the Masters had followed—the road to heightened powers and the toll that journey extracted. Ever since the Masters left, Cabell and his young assistant, Rem, had been trying to replicate Zor's achievements. But Cabell was now beginning to believe that the process was more one of mind than of matter, and that Protoculture would never be scientifically conjured from the Flowers—it had to be *willed* from them.

As Lang listened to Cabell's assessment of the Masters, he found himself growing weary and almost bemused by the Expeditionary mission's ironic accomplishment: in leaving Earth behind, they had left the door wide open for the Masters' arrival. It occurred to him that peace would never have been possible with such a race, and he could only shudder at the thought of Earth in the incapable hands of Leonard and the Army of the Southern Cross.

Once in the fold-generator hold, the language of pure science replaced the grunts and glottal stops of the Tiresian tongue. The computer was their interpreter now, and as

Cabell inspected the generators, he and Lang began to communicate with mathematics and schematic appraisals. Lang was amazed at how quickly the Tiresian was able to adapt and *reshape* his thinking to fit the demands of Human artificial-intelligence systems.

"But you have the necessary Protoculture reserves for a fold," Cabell said after a long while. "Enough for a flotilla of ships, in fact. All that's lacking is sufficient fuel for the Reflex drives." He saw Lang's bewildered look, and quickly created a program that could illustrate his ideas. Once or twice he called on Exedore to define a word or phrase.

Lang watched as a series of esoteric holographic displays took shape on the screen. He studied them a moment and offered Cabell a restrained smile. "Now I understand."

A fold required an all-important interaction between Protoculture and the fuels that powered the Reflex drives themselves, an interaction his teams would never had guessed.

"But what you have here would call for a magnetic monopole ore, Cabell."

The Tiresian looked impatient. "Well, of course. How else *could* it be done?"

"But we haven't the equipment necessary to create this much material," Lang told him. "And even if we did, it would require more time—"

"Nonsense," Cabell said dismissively. "You have all the ore you need right there."

Lang and Exedore followed Cabell's finger out the viewport.

"Fantoma?"

"You don't remember a time when the Zentraedi were miners, Exedore?" Cabell asked.

Exedore seemed almost embarrassed by the question. "I

do, Cabell. But we were never told what it was we were mining."

Cabell turned to Lang. "The base may be difficult for you to utilize since it was sized to suit the Zentraedi; but the ore is still there for the taking."

Lang stepped to the viewport and looked long and hard at the giant planet's jade-colored crescent. Then, as his eyes found diminutive Tirol, he recalled a premonition he had had long before the SDF-3's departure from Earth-space. He thought of the SDF-3's sizing chamber, and of Breetai's small team of Micronized Battlepod warriors.

Exedore was standing alongside him now. "But will we have enough time, sir?"

Lang said, "We have nothing but time."

The lights in the sky are stars, Jonathan Wolff told himself short of the tunnel entrance. He had dismounted the Hovertank and was gazing up into Tirol's incomparable night. But there was at least one light up there that wasn't a star, and he made a wish on it.

Minmei was somewhere on that unblinking presence he identified as the SDF-3, and the wish was meant to ascend to her heart. Wolff had hardly been able to keep her from his thoughts these past two days; even in the midst of that first day's battle he would recall her face or the fragrance of her hair when she had come to the dropship hold to wish him luck, to embrace him. He wondered how he had allowed her to take hold of him like this, and considered for a moment that she might have *witched* herself into his mind. Because it was out of control all of a sudden, a flirtation he had played on the off-chance, never figuring she would respond. And what of Catherine? he asked himself. Was she, too, staring up into evening's light, her arm around the thin shoulder of their only son, and sending him a wish across the galaxy? While he had already forgotten, broken the pledge he had promised to stick to this time, so they could have the second chance their marriage so desperately needed.

Odd thoughts to be thinking on such a night, Wolff mused.

"All set, sir," the lieutenant's voice reported from behind him.

Wolff took a quick breath and swung around. "I want it to go by the numbers, Lieutenant," he warned. "Two teams, no surprises. Now, where's our voice?"

The lieutenant shouted, "Quist!" and a short, solid-looking ranger approached and snapped to.

"You stick to me like glue, Corporal," Wolff told him. "Every time I put my hand out I expect to find you on the end of it, got that?"

"Yes, sir."

Wolff gave Quist the once-over. "All right, let's hit it."

The lieutenant got the teams moving through the smoke toward the subterranean corridors. It hadn't taken a genius to locate the entry once they had gotten a clear fix on where the Beta from Skull had touched down. And that crazy kid, Baker, had a good memory if nothing else, Wolff had to concede; his recall of the ruined buildings in the area bordered on the uncanny.

Wolff signaled for everyone to hold up at the entrance. He peered down into the darkness, then took a look behind him, where four Hovertanks were guarding the rear. The corridor was tall and wide, but not big enough to accommodate a mecha. Stairways, secondary corridors, and some kind of huge lenslike medallions could be discerned from up here.

Wolff found himself thinking back to the journals his grandfather had kept during a minor Indo-Chinese war few people remembered. Back then, Jack Wolff and a handful of tunnel rats used to go into these things with flashlights and gunpowder handguns. Wolff checked the safety on his blaster and had to laugh: his grandfather wrote about the booby traps, the spiders and rats. Today it would be mindless feline robot drones and a host of other stuff they probably hadn't even seen yet. But all in all it was the same old thing: a sucker's tour of the unknown.

"Bring those Amblers in," Wolff ordered.

Two squat, bipedal Robosearchlights moved up to throw intense light into the hole.

Wolff and his Pack began to follow them down.

CHAPTER
THIRTEEN

If Exedore had an Invid counterpart, it would have to be the scientist [sic], Tesla, for no other of the Regis's children was possessed of such a wide-ranging intellect and personality. It is interesting to note, however, that although fashioned by the Regis, Tesla had much more of the Regent in his makeup. One has to wonder if the Regis, taking Zor as her only model, mistakenly assigned certain characteristics to males, and others to females. Marlene, Sera, and Corg—her human child—immediately come to mind. Was she, then, in some sense culpable for fostering the Regent's devolved behavior?

Bloom Nesterfig, *The Social Organization of the Invid*

IT WAS TESLA WHO TOLD THE REGIS ABOUT THE TROUBLE on Tirol. He was one of the Regent's "scientists"—how she laughed at this notion!—and currently the commander of the Karbarran starship that was transporting life-forms back to the Regent's zoo on Optera. Tesla had been something of a favorite child, but the Regis had become suspicious of his ostensibly metaphysical strivings, and had nothing but distrust for him now that he had allied himself with her estranged husband. Tesla reminded her of the Regent; there was the same burning intensity in his black eyes, the same distention and blush to his feelers. He had no details about the situation on Tirol, other than to note that the Regent had dispatched two additional warships from Optera to see to some new emergency.

"So he's gotten himself into another fix," the Regis sneered.

"A possible entanglement, Your Highness," Tesla replied, offering her a somewhat obligatory and half-hearted salute. "A complication, perhaps. But hardly a 'fix.'"

The two were on Praxis, where a shuttle from the Karbarran ship had put down to take on supplies and specimens. The starship itself, a medley of modular drives and transport units from a dozen worlds, was in orbit near the Praxian moon; it was crewed by slaves, ursine creatures native to Karbarra, a world rich in the Protoculture Peat that fueled the ship.

A sentry announced that one of Tesla's lieutenants wished to speak with him. The Regis granted permission, and the lieutenant entered a moment later. Two Praxians, cuffed at wrist and ankle, followed. They were ravishing creatures, the Regis thought, appraising the duo Tesla had handpicked for the Regent's zoo. Tall, Tiresioid females with thick, lustrous pelts and strategic swaths of primitive costume to offset their smooth nakedness. The Regis confessed to a special fondness for the Praxians and their forested, fertile planet; but Praxis held even greater charms in its volcanic depths. Tesla, however, was unaware of the Genesis Pits she had fashioned here—her underground experiments in creative evolution.

"Shall I take these two to the ship?" Tesla's lieutenant asked.

As Tesla approached the females to look them over more closely, the taller of the two began to spit and curse at him, straining wildly against the cuffs that bound her. The Enforcer turned to silence her and took a bite on the hand.

Ravishing, the Regis told herself, *but warriors to the last*.

Ultimately the lieutenant brought a weapon to bear on the pair; stunned, they collapsed to their knees and whimpered.

Tesla nodded and adopted the folded-arm posture characteristic of his group. "Yes, they'll do fine," he told his soldier. "And see that they're well caged."

The Regis made a scoffing sound when the females had been led out. "My husband's need for *pets*. Instead of furthering his own evolution, he chooses to surround himself with captives—to bask in his self-deluded superiority." She glared at Tesla, finding his form repugnant, in so many ways inferior to the very beings his ship carried like so much stock. "So what are you bringing him this time, *servant*?"

Tesla ignored the slur. "Feel free to inspect our cargo, Your Highness. We have choice samples from Karbarra, Spheris, Garuda, Peryton, and now Praxis. A brief stopover on Haydon IV, and our cages will be full."

The Regis whirled on the scientist. "Haydon IV?" There was a sudden note of concern in her voice. "Have you given clear thought to the possible consequences of such an action?"

Tesla shrugged his massive shoulders. "What could go wrong, Your Highness? Haydon IV is our world now, is it not?"

Haydon IV belongs to no one, the Regis kept to herself. Captives aside, Tesla would be lucky to leave that world alive.

Her husband was about to make a serious mistake, but she could not bring herself to intervene.

* * *

The raucous sound of a static-spiced squawkbox woke Janice from dreams of electric sheep. One eye opened, she spied Minmei on her knees across the room trying to adjust the radio's volume.

"Too late," Janice called out.

Minmei swung around, surprised, fingertips to her lips. "I didn't mean to wake you."

Janice sat up and yawned. "I'm sure." She'd fallen off an hour ago, just after Lynn had left their new quarters for parts unknown. "What is that—a transceiver?"

"No one will tell me anything about Jonathan. This is a kind of, uh, unscrambler. I thought I could pick up some combat reports."

Janice stood up to get a better look at the radio and its decoder feed. "Where'd you get this, Lynn?"

"Promise not to tell?"

Janice looked around the room, calling attention to their confinement. "Who am I going to tell?"

"A woman who works for Dr. Lang got it for me. I explained the situation."

"Stardom does have its advantages, doesn't it?" Janice kneeled down next to Minmei and reached a finger out to readjust the radio's tuner. In a minute she located the com net's frequency.

"—neral Edwards and the Ghost Squadron are already on their way, over," someone was updating. After several seconds of static a second voice said, "That's good news, com two. We've lost Wolff—"

Minmei's gasp erased the next few words; then Janice succeeded in quieting her. "Listen, Lynn, just listen."

". . . had him for a while, but we're getting nothing now. Probably that force field. Everything was roses up till then. No sign of enemy activity."

"You see," Janice said. Minmei was still upset, but hopeful again. "It'll be all right, I promise."

Trembling, Minmei shut off the receiver and got to her feet. "I can't listen to it," she said, wringing her hands. "I just can't think about the horrible things he must be facing." She collapsed, crying, into Janice's open arms.

In the nave of the Royal Hall, the Invid brain looked as though it might succumb to a stroke at any moment. Cells were flashing out one after another as power continued to be shunted to the force shield and energy reserves were depleted. A dozen or so soldiers stood motionless, awaiting the brain's command.

Obsim, too, was on the verge of panic, convinced now that the Regent meant to abandon him there. Looking frightened and desperate, he paced back and forth in front of the brain's bubble chamber under the expressionless gaze of his Enforcer unit.

"Don't watch me like that!" he shouted, suddenly aware of their eyes on him. "Who let the Tiresians escape? It wasn't me, I can tell you that much. Don't I have enough to do already? Do I have to do *everything* myself?" He waved a four-fingered fist at them. "Heads are going to roll, I promise you!"

Obsim tried to avoid thinking about the punishment the Regent would have in store for him. A one-way trip to the Genesis Pits, perhaps, for quick devolvement. Nothing like a little reverse ontogeny to bring someone around. Obsim had seen others go through it; he recalled the sight of them crawling from the pits like land crabs—obscene representations of an evolutionary past the Invid had never lived through, a form that existed only in the shape and design of the Pincer Ships and Shock Troopers.

Obsim stopped pacing to confront the brain.

"Situation," he demanded.

The living computer struggled to revive itself; it floated listlessly in the middle depths of the tank, dull and discolored. Obsim repeated his command.

"Intruders have entered the subterranean vaults and corridors," the brain managed at last.

"Show me!" Obsim barked, fighting to keep his fear in check. "Let the Inorganics be my eyes."

An image began to take shape in the interior of the communicator sphere; gradually it resolved, albeit distorted, as if through a fish-eye lens. Obsim saw a small group of armed invaders moving through the corridors on foot. There were males and females among them, outfitted in helmets, body armor, visual and audio scanners. The Inorganic remained in its place of concealment and allowed them to pass by unharmed.

"There is a second group," the computer announced. "Closer than the first. In the area where the Tiresians' transmissions originated."

That place had not been found; the Inorganics had instead given chase to the Tiresians themselves.

"They entered the way the others left," Obsim speculated. "Could they be in league?"

The brain assessed the probability and flashed the results in the communicator sphere.

Obsim made a disgusted sound. "As I feared. They must be stopped."

"Activating the Inorganics will substantially weaken the shield," the brain said, second-guessing Obsim's command.

"Do it anyway." The scientist straightened his thick neck, allowing him to regard the room's distant ceiling.

"Let them waste their firepower battering us from above, while we destroy their forces below."

"Puppies?" Wolff repeated, exchanging puzzled glances with the radioman. "Ask him to clarify."

Quist listened for a moment. "She says they look like little sheepdogs, sir, except there's something funny about their eyes and they've got some kind of horns. Sounds like there's a whole bunch of 'em."

"You can hear them?"

"Yes, sir."

Wolff pressed the headset to his ear and heard a chorus of shrill barks. "Sounds like they're crying," he commented. "Verify their position. Tell them to sit tight."

Aware that the external links were down, Wolff sent a runner back to the entrance, then gave the signal for the team to move out. His group had encountered nothing but mile after mile of corridor and serviceway, with the occasional cavernous room to break the monotony. By all accounts they were well beneath the Royal Hall, but they had yet to locate a way up. The B team, however, had wandered into a tight maze of even smaller tunnels, and were now in what their lieutenant described as a database lab. That's where they found the puppies.

Half an hour later the two teams reunited.

It was indeed a computer room, consoles and screens galore, but the lieutenant's "puppies" were anything but. The creatures remained huddled together in one corner of the lab, screaming their sad song, loath, it appeared, to leave their spot.

"Sir, I tried to pick one of them up and it just seemed to disappear right out of my arms," the lieutenant told Wolff.

He gave her a dubious look and was about to try for

himself when the voice of one of the corridor sentries rang out.

"We've got movement, people! From all directions!"

Wolff studied the motion-detector display briefly. There was a wider corridor two hundred yards left of the lab that led almost straight to the entrance, with a two or three jags thrown in. He dispatched a second runner with instructions for the tankers, and began to hurry everyone along toward the corridor.

"The . . . *things*, sir, do we leave them?"

Wolff glanced into the room at the Pollinators' white-shag pile. "They're probably just Tirol's way of saying 'rat.' Now let's move!"

Delivered into the upper reaches of Tirol's envelope only moments before, the Ghost Squadron dropped out of Tiresia's dawn like brilliant tongues of flame, half to batter away at the Royal Hall's evaporating shield, while Edwards's elite rushed in to follow the Wolff Pack's trail. Edwards had Cabell's map of that subterranean maze in hand now, and was determined to get to the Invid brain before anyone else.

The commander of the Hovertanks waiting by the crater entrance to the corridors didn't know what to think as he watched General Edwards leap from VT's cockpit and commence what looked like angry strides in his direction. He jumped down from his own turret cockpit and ordered everyone to attention. But it was obvious in an instant that Edwards wasn't interested in formalities or honorifics.

"What's Wolff's position?" Edwards demanded, pulling off his helmet and gloves.

A lieutenant ran forward and produced the sketchy map Wolff had sent back with one of the runners. Edwards snatched the thing away before the officer could lay it out.

"They're about half a mile in, General," the lieutenant said, while Edwards began comparing Wolff's map to the one Cabell had drawn.

"Who was the last man in there?" Edwards asked, preoccupied.

A young corporal presented herself and articulated a summary of the present situation. "The colonel has pulled back to a position . . . here," she said, indicating a corridor junction on the cruder map. "The colonel hopes to lure the enemy along this corridor—"

"It's plain what the colonel proposes to do, Corporal," the squadron commander said before Edwards could turn on the woman.

Edwards studied the maps a moment longer, then grunted in a satisfied way, and began to suit up in the gear one of his number brought over. "I want you to see to it that no one follows us in there, Captain—*no one*, is that understood." Menacingly, Edwards flicked his rifle's selector to full auto and all but brandished the weapon.

"Understood, General, we'll hold them here," the captain responded, trying his best not to have it come out sounding confused.

Edwards tapped the man roughly on the shoulder as he stepped past him. "Good for you." He waved his twelve forward and they disappeared into the floodlit entrance.

Five minutes along, Edwards pulled Colonel Adams aside to give him special instructions. Again they consulted the Tiresian's map, and Edwards pointed out the tunnels that would lead directly to the heart of the Royal Hall.

"Wolff is closer to the Invid brain than he probably realizes," Edwards began. "And if he can break through whatever it is they're throwing against him, he's going to find the way in. Detail three men and make certain that doesn't happen. Give him rear fire if you have to, anything that'll pin him down." Edwards showed Adams the route he would be taking. "I'm going around him, but I need some extra time."

Adams glanced at the corridor's smooth walls and ceiling. "Maybe we can arrange a cave-in for him."

"Do whatever it takes," Edwards said harshly, repocketing the map. "It'll be no one's loss if he doesn't make it out of here."

Elsewhere in the corridors, Wolff had ordered his Pack to open fire. They couldn't see what they were shooting at, but the energy hyphens the enemy was returning were similar to the drone bursts they had faced on the surface. There was nothing in the way of cover, so everyone was either facedown on the floor, or plastered flat against the walls, retreating by odd and even counts through stroboscopic light, blasts of heat, and earsplitting explosions.

Backed around the first jag in the maze, they had a moment to catch their breath, while a horizontal hail of fire flew past them down the central corridor. In response to a tap on the shoulder from the radioman, Wolff raised the faceshield of his helmet. They had reestablished traffic with the Hovertank command.

"We must be outside the field already," Wolff said.

"Negative, sir. Command reports the barrier is softening. The Ghost Squadron's hammering it to death."

"Edwards, huh? Guess we shouldn't be choosy."

Quist smiled. "No, sir. The rest of his team—"

"We got troubles, Colonel," the team's point interrupted breathlessly, motioning up the corridor. "I'm picking up movement. They're boxing us in."

Wolff shifted his gaze between the storm off to their left

and the corridor ahead. "But how . . . They would've had to pass the tanks—"

"Incoming!" someone yelled, and the corridor ceiling took two oblique hits.

Wolff and his team tried to meld with the floor as fire and explosive debris rained down all around them. The ceiling sustained two follow-up hits before he could even lift his head. Then he heard Quist say, "It's coming down!" just when everything began to crumble . . .

"It's no use," Rick announced in the dark, sitting straight up in bed.

Lisa stirred beside him and reached out a hand to find the light pad. He was already out of bed by the time the ceiling spots came on, hands on hips, pacing. Lisa said nothing, deciding to wait until he had walked off some of his frustration. She was exhausted and in no mood for a midnight support session, let alone an argument. Even so, she had managed only an hour of half sleep herself, expecting this very scene.

Rick had been impossible since the Tiresians' capture, and his behavior seemed to be having a kind of contagious effect on everyone around him. Suddenly there was an atmosphere of hopelessness, a sense that the situation had become untenable. Lives had been lost, the spacefold generators had been damaged, the very Masters they had come so far to meet were on their way to Earth . . . For Lisa the events of the past few days had given rise to a peculiar mix of thoughts and feelings; it was not unlike a time ten years ago, when the crew of the SDF-1 had been thrust overnight into a whirlwind of terror. But she refused to permit herself to relive those moments of dread and anticipation, and was determined to steer clear of behavioral ruts. And much to her surprise, she found that she had discovered the strength to meet all the fear and challenges head on, some inner reserve that not only allowed her to *maintain*, but to conquer and forge ahead. She wanted to believe that Rick had made the same discovery, but it was almost as if he had willingly surrendered to the past, and was actually desirous of that retro-gravitation. This from the man who had been so take-charge these past six years, who had devoted himself to the SDF-3's construction and its crucial mission.

"Rick, you've got to get some rest," she said at last. "This isn't doing either of us any good."

It seemed to be the only conversation they could have anymore, and she knew exactly what he was about to say.

"You just don't understand, do you? I *need* to be doing more than just standing around waiting for things to happen. I have to get back where I belong—even if that means resigning my command."

She met Rick's gaze and held it until he turned away. "You're right. Maybe I don't understand you anymore. I mean, I understand your *frustrations*, but you're going to have to tell me why you need to risk your life out there. Haven't you proved yourself a hundred times over, Rick?" Lisa threw up her hands.

"It's my duty to be with my team."

"It's your duty to *command*," she said, raising her voice. "It's not your duty to get yourself killed!"

Rick had an answer ready for delivery when all at once Lisa's com tone sounded. She leaned over, hit the switch, and said, "Admiral Hayes."

It was the bridge: scanners had picked up two Invid troop carriers closing fast on the fortress.

Rick saw Lisa blanch; agitated, she pushed her hair back from her face. He was about to go over to her when his own intercom erupted.

"Tell General Reinhardt to meet me in the Room," Rick

said, responding to the brief message. He switched off, and rushed to the wardrobe, pulling out one of his old flight suits.

"I'm on my way," he heard Lisa say into the com.

She watched him suit up in silence; there were tears in her eyes when he bent over to kiss her good-bye.

"I have to do it," he told her.

Lisa turned away from him. "Expect me to do the same."

FOURTEEN

We have a desperate new mission: to mine enough of Fantoma's mysterious ore to rebuild the fortress's damaged spacefold generators, and journey to the other side of the galaxy to save our beleaguered world from destruction at the hands of the Robotech Masters. If this mission sounds suspiciously like the old mission, it's because it is the old mission, played backwards. I am growing weary of the ironies; I am growing weary of the whole thing.

The collected Journals of Admiral Rick Hunter

THE CLAM-SHAPED INVID TROOP CARRIERS REMANI-fested in Fantoma's brightside space, using the giant's rings for ECM cover and yawning more than a thousand Pincer Ships into the void, while the Earthforces' superdimensional fortress raised its energy shields and swung itself from stationary orbit. As the fortress's secondary batteries traversed and ranged in, teams of Alpha and first-generation Veritech fighters streamed from the launch bays. Inside the mile-long ship, men and women answered the call of klaxons and alert sirens, racing to battle stations and readying themselves in dozens of command posts and gun turrets. Scanners linked to the Tactical Information Center's big boards swept and probed; computers tied in to those same systems assessed, analyzed, executed, and distributed a steady flow of data; techs and processors bent to their assigned tasks, requesting updates and entering commands, hands and fingers a blur as they flew across keyboards, decks, and consoles.

On the enemy's side, things were much less complicated: pilots listened and obeyed, hurling themselves against the Humans' war machine with a passionless intensity, a blind obedience, a violent frenzy...

"Are you sure you want to go through with this?" Max Sterling asked Rick over the tac net. Rick's image was on the VT's right commo screen. Miriya was on the left one. There was still time to turn back.

"Positive, Skull Leader," Rick responded. "And I don't want either of you babysitting me."

"Now, why would we want to do that?" Miriya said.

Rick made a face. "Well, that's what everybody else is trying to do."

Max made light of his friend's plight, but at the same time was fully aware of the concern he felt. He had no worries about Rick's combat skills—he had kept his hand in all these years. But Rick seemed to have forgotten that out here stray thoughts were as dangerous as annihilation discs. *Nothing extraneous in mind or body,* Max was tempted to remind him. Any pilot, no matter how good he or she might be, had to keep those words in mind; it was as much a warning as it was a code. Mechamorphosis was a serious matter even under optimum conditions; but in space combat it meant the difference between life and death.

Max took a long look at the cockpit displays; the Invid crab-ships were just coming into range. The field was so packed the enemy registered as a white blur on his radar screen. Signatures and targeting information came up on one of the peripherals.

"Block party of bandits," Max said evenly, "nine o'clock clear around to three. ETAs on closure are coming in . . ."

"Roger, Skull Leader," Rick radioed back. "Talk about your target-rich environment. They're going to be all over us."

Max could hear a certain excitement, an *enthusiasm*, in Rick's tone.

"We've got a job to do," he advised. "Let's just take them as they come. Nothing fancy. Go for target lock."

Rick acknowledged. "Ready to engage."

Max tightened his hand on the HOTAS. He had visuals on the lead ships now, pincers gleaming in starlight.

An instant later the cold blackness of space was holed by a thousand lights. Death dropped its starting flag and the slaughter recommenced.

Jonathan Wolff had yet to see a finish line for the hellish race his team was running in Tiresia's cruel underground. Four had died instantly in the corridor's collapse, and two more had been pinned under the superheated debris; the rest of the team was huddled on top of each other at the junction, throwing everything they had around the corner. But there was something to be thankful for: the cave-in had only partially sealed off their escape route. Moreover, while the drones were continuing their slow advance, whatever had hit them from behind was gone.

"I'm not picking up any movement, sir," the pointman was shouting above the clamor of the weapons.

Wolff wiped bits of cooled metal from his bodysuit and regarded the mass that had almost buried him. It was the same smooth, ceramiclike material that made up Tiresia's surface streets and many of the city's buildings. Some ferrocrete analogue, he guessed.

A corpsman was seeing to the wounded.

Wolff motioned to Quist and asked in hand signals if they still had contact with the tanks.

The radioman nodded.

"Advise them of our situation and tell them we need support," Wolff said into Quist's ear. "I want to see a fire team down here in ten minutes. And I don't care if they have to blast their way in with the tanks."

Quist crouched down along the wall and began to repeat it word for word. Wolff moved to the medic's side. The wounded soldier was a young woman on temporary duty from one of Grant's units. She couldn't have been older than eighteen, and she was torn up pretty badly. *Powers*, Wolff recalled.

He reached down to brush a strand of damp hair from her face; she returned a weak but stoic smile. Wolff gritted his teeth and stood up, infuriated. He spoke Minmei's name in a whisper and hurried to the junction, his handgun drawn.

Deeper in the maze, Edwards had had his first glimpse of the enemy; but he hadn't stopped to puzzle out or catalog just what it was he had killed. His team was simply firing its way through corridor after corridor, stepping over the bodies and smoking shells their weapons leveled. Hellcats, Scrim, Crann—it made no difference to Edwards; he was closing on the access stairway to the nave of the Royal Hall, and that was all that mattered.

Colonel Adam's splinter group had rejoined the main team after throwing some red-hot rear fire Wolff's way. If they hadn't been entirely successful in burying the Pack alive, Adam's team had at least seen to it that Wolff was no longer in the running for the grand prize, the Invid brain.

Edwards, at point with a gun in each hand, was the first to see the jagged trench Obsim's enforcers had opened in the floor of the Hall. He had no notion of its purpose, but he guessed that the narrow band of overhead light was coming from a room close to the nave, perhaps even adjacent to it. He waved the team to a halt and spent a moment contemplating his options. Surely the brain was aware of their presence, unless the Ghost's bombing runs had given it too much else to think about. Even so, Edwards decided, the enemy was down to the dregs of its force. The things he killed in the corridors were easy prey, and if the Tiresian's word could be trusted, that was all the more reason to assume the brain was preoccupied.

He asked himself whether the brain would expect him to come up through the breach. It would be a difficult and hazardous ascent. But then, why would they have trenched the Hall's floor if they knew about the stairway? He forced any decision from his mind and fell back, allowing his instincts free reign.

And something told him to push on.

Five minutes later the team was creeping up the steep stairway Cabell had described, and Edwards's hand had found the panel stud that would trigger the door. He gave the team the go sign and slammed the switch with the heel of his fist. They poured up and out of the tunnels wailing like banshees, rolling and tearing across the nave's hard floor, lobbing concussion grenades and loosing bursts of death.

Two rows of Invid soldiers who were waiting for them to come through the nave's front entrance were caught by surprise and chopped down in seconds. But two Shock Troopers stepped out of nowhere and began dumping annihilation discs into the hole, frying a quarter of the team before the rest could bring the ships down with a barrage of scanner shots. One of the ships cracked open like an egg, spilling a thick green wash across the floor; the other came apart in an explosion that decapitated the lieutenant.

The nave was filled with fire, smoke, and pandemonium now, but Edwards moved through it like a cat, closing on the brain's towering bubble chamber while the team mopped up. Two seven-foot-tall sentries came at him, spewing bolts of orange flame from their forearm cannons, but he managed to throw himself clear. At the same time he heard the simultaneous discharge of two rocket launchers, and covered himself as the projectiles found their mark.

Edwards was on his feet and back on track before the explosions subsided. Out of the corner of his eye he caught sight of an unarmed robed figure making a mad dash for the brain. The alien started babbling away and waving its arms in a panicked fashion, as if to plead with Edwards to cease fire. Edwards held up his hand and the nave grew eerily silent, save for Obsim's rantings and the crackle of fires.

"What's it saying?" Major Benson asked.

Edwards told them all to keep quiet. "Go ahead, alien, make your pitch."

A rush of sounds left Obsim's mouth, but it was the brain that spoke. In English.

"Invaders, listen to me: you must not destroy the brain. The brain lives and is a power unto itself. Your purpose and desires are understood, and the brain can see to your needs."

Again Edwards had to tell everyone to cut the chatter. The tall Invid continued to mouth sounds from its snaillike head, which was bobbing up and down at the end of a long, thick neck.

"Behold," the brain translated, as the communicator sphere began to glow. "Your people are at this very moment battling our troops near the rings of Tirol's mother-world."

The communicator showed them a scene of fierce fighting, Pincer Ships and Veritechs locked in mortal combat.

Obsim made a high-pitched sound and swung around to face Edwards, hands tucked in his sleeves. "The brain can put an end to it."

Edwards stared at the alien, then leveled his weapons at the bubble chamber. "Showtime."

From the command chair's elevated position on the SDF-3 bridge, Lisa had a clear view of the battle's distant light show, countless strobelike explosions erupting across an expanse of local space like so many short-lived novas. The Veritech teams were successful at keeping most of the Invid ships away from the fortress, and those few that had broken through were taken out with the in-close weapons systems. But the silent flares, the laser-array bolts, and annihilation discs detailed only half the story; for the rest one would have to turn to the tac net and its cacophony of commands and requests, its warnings and imprecations and prayers, its cries and deathscreams.

Lisa had promised to keep it all at arm's length, to maintain a strategic distance, much as she was doing with the fortress. Resolute, she voiced her commands in a clipped, almost severe tone, and when she watched those lights, it was with a deliberate effort to force their meaning from her thoughts.

An update from one of the duty stations brought her swiveling around now to face the threat board: the two motherships had changed course. Lisa called for position and range.

"Approach vectors on-screen, sir," said an enlisted rating tech. "They're coming straight at us."

"The Skull team requests permission to engage."

Lisa whirled around. "Negative! They're to pull back at once."

She turned again to study a heads-up monitor and ordered a course correction. Reinhardt's voice was booming through the squawkboxes, his bearded face on one of the screens. He asked for a second correction, a subtle maneuver to reposition the main gun.

"Coming around to zero-zero-niner, sir. Standing by..."

"Picking up strong EV readings. We're being scanned and targeted."

"Get me Lang," Lisa ordered.

Lang addressed her from a peripheral screen; he had anticipated her question. "We've shunted power from the shields to the main gun, but we're still well protected." At the same time, she heard Reinhardt say, "Prepare to fire on my command."

"Has the Skull pulled out?"

"Uh, checking..."

"Quickly!" she barked.

"Affirmative," the tech stammered. "They're clear."

"On my mark—" Reinhardt started to say.

Suddenly two brilliant flashes flowered into life in front of the ship, throwing blinding light through the viewport. Caught in the grip of the exposions, the fortress was shaken forcefully enough to toss techs from their stations and send them clear across the bridge.

Lisa's neck felt as though it had snapped. She put one hand to the back of her head, and asked if everyone was all right. Sirens somewhere off in the ship had changed tone; the fortress had sustained damage.

"What happened?" Lisa said as reports poured in.

"No trace of the ships, sir."

"God, it's like something *vaporized* them . . ."

Lisa watched in awe as the light show began to wink out.

"What's going on out there—has the enemy disengaged?"

The threat-board tech scratched his head. "No, sir; er, yes, sir. That is, the VT teams report all enemy ships inactive. They're dead in space."

The tech on the SDF-3 bridge wasn't the only one scratching his head. In a corridor fifty feet beneath Tiresia's Royal Hall, Jonathan Wolff was doing the same thing.

"They just stopped firing," one of the Pack was saying.

Certainly no one was about to argue with that or be anything less than overjoyed, but the question remained: *why?*

Wolff poked his head around the corner of the corridor like some of the others were doing, and saw half-a-dozen bipedal Inorganics stopped not ten years from the junction. And not simply stopped, but shut down—frozen. Presently, everyone who could stand was out in the middle of the central corridor gaping at the silent drones; it was the first time any of them had had a chance to inspect the things up close, and they found themselves relieved enough to comment on their remarkable design. Wolff, however, put a quick end to it.

The requested fire team had arrived without incident from the other side of the collapse. Wolff sent the wounded back, along with most of the original squad—it was looking better for Powers—and pushed on toward the Royal Hall. The field command post had yet to hear word one from Edwards's team.

They remained cautious and alert as they regained the ground they had surrendered. Wolff led them past the computer room and on into a confusing warren of tunnels and ducts. Along the way they passed dozens of Inorganics in the same state of suspended animation. But at last they came to the trench Edwards had seen earlier, and instinctively Wolff knew they were close to reaching the center.

"It's blue smoke and mirrors," Edwards sneered as the image in the communicator sphere de-rezzed. He had seen the explosions that wiped out the two troop carriers, but remained unconvinced. "You could be running home movies for all I know."

Obsim made a puzzled gesture and turned to the brain.

"You have a suspicious mind, Invader." The synthesized voice had a raspy sound to it now, as though fatigued.

"That's right, Mister Wizard, and I'm also the one holding a gun to your head." Edwards half turned to one of his men. "I want immediate confirmation on what we just saw. See if you can raise anyone."

The radioman moved off and Edwards continued. "But if you *are* on the level, I've got to say I'm impressed. The brain is certainly far too valuable to destroy—but then again, it's far too dangerous to remain operative."

Obsim showed Edwards his palms, then fumbled to open a concealed access panel in the bubble chamber's hourglass-shaped base.

"The brain can be deactivated. It can be yours to command."

Interested, Edwards stepped forward, brandishing the weapon.

"Go ahead, alien."

Obsim pulled two dermatrode leads from the panel and placed them flat against the center of his head; his fingers meanwhile tapped a command sequence into the panel's ten-key touchpad. At the same time, the brain seemed to compress as it settled toward the bottom of the chamber. After a moment Obsim reversed the process, causing an effervescent rush inside the tank as the brain revived.

"Again," said Edwards, and Obsim repeated it. Then it was Edwards's turn to try, while Colonel Adams held a gun to Obsim's snout. Edwards got it right on the first take; the brain was asleep.

Edwards shut the panel and stood up, grinning at the alien. "You've been a most gracious host." Without taking his eyes off Obsim, he yelled, "Do we have that confirmation, soldier?"

"Affirmative," came the reply.

"Waste him," Edwards said to Adams.

The burst blew out the Invid scientist's brain; the body collapsed in a heap, Obsim's once-white robes drenched in grccn.

"Wargasm." Adams laughed.

Edwards regarded each of his men individually; thc gazc from his single eye said much more than any verbal warning could.

Just then, Human voices could be heard on the staircase. Edwards and his men swung around, weapons armed, only to find Jonathan Wolff crawling cautiously from the hole.

Wolff took a look around the room, as his team followed him out. There were two devastated Shock Trooper ships and twenty or more Invid corpses. Wolff had seen the charred remains of what looked like four men on the steps. Now he focused his attention on the bubble chamber.

"This the thing the Tiresians were talking about, sir?"

"That's it, Colonel," Edwards said.

Wolff glanced down at Obsim, then at Edwards. He had questions for the general, questions about what had gone on in the corridors and what had gone on here, but he sensed it wasn't the right time—not with Edwards's team looking as though they weren't full yet. Ultimately, he said, "Too bad I didn't arrive sooner, sir."

"You're lucky you didn't," Adams told him with a sly smile. "It was a real horror show."

"Yeah," Wolff mused, watching Edwards's men trade looks, "I can imagine."

Edwards broke the subsequent silence by ordering his radioman to make contact with the ship.

Edwards was jubilant. "Tell them the mission was a complete success."

Without warning, he slapped Wolff on the back.

"Smile, Colonel—you're a hero!"

CHAPTER
FIFTEEN

*It was without question a mind-boost for [Edwards], compara-
ble to the one Dr. Emil Lang had received while reconning the
SDF-1. And in the same way Lang became almost instantly conversant with Zor's science, Robotechnology, Edwards became
conversant with the lusts and drives of the Invid Regent. This,
however, was not engrammation, but amplification. Edwards and
the Regent were analogues of one another: scarred, vengeful, and
dangerous beings.*

Constance Wildman, *When Evil Had Its Day:
A Biography of T. R. Edwards*

THE BATTLE WAS OVER AND AN UNEASY CALM PRE-
vailed; no one aboard the SDF-3 was sure how long the lull
would last, but if the Robotech War had taught them anything, it was that they should make the most of tranquil
interludes.

None dared call it peace.

One by one the inert Invid ships were destroyed, after it
was determined that the pilots were all dead. Dr. Lang and
Cabell speculated that the living computer, in addition to
vaporizing the troop carriers and shutting down the Inorganics, had issued some sort of blanket suicide directive.
Many among the RDF found this difficult to accept, but the
explanation was strengthened by Cabell's recounting of

equally puzzling and barbarous acts the Invid had carried out. On the moon's surface, a building-to-building search was under way, and most of Tiresia's humanoid population had been freed. The hundreds of drones that littered Tiresia's subterranean passageways remained lifeless; one day soon that labyrinth would be sealed up, along with the Royal Hall and the sleeping brain itself. But that would not be before Cabell had had a chance to show Lang around, or before the Pollinators had been rescued and removed.

There was something of a mutual-admiration society in the works between Lang and the bearded Tiresian scientist. And while it was true that the Expeditionary mission had "liberated" Tirol, it was questionable whether that could have been achieved without Cabell and Rem's intelligence. More to the point, Cabell's importance in the work that lay ahead for the mission's robotech teams was beyond dispute. Lang had taken every opportunity to press him for details of the mining operation, and was eagerly awaiting the RDF's clearance for a recon landing on Fantoma. Earth's survival depended on their being able to mine enough ore to rebuild the SDF-3's damaged engines, and to fold home before the Masters arrived.

During the course of the discussions, Lang learned something of Tirol's gradual swing toward militarism in the years following Zor's great discoveries. Cabell spoke of a short-lived but wonderful time when *exploration* had been his people's main concern. Indeed, the Zentraedi themselves were originally created to serve those ends as miners, not as the galactic warriors they would eventually become. The defoliation of Optera, the Invid homeworld, had been their first directive under the reconfigured imperative. There followed a succession of conquests and police actions, and, ultimately, warfare against the very creatures whose world they had destroyed.

Then they had traveled halfway across the galaxy to die . . .

As Lang listened he began to feel a kind of sympathy for the Invid; it was obvious there were mysteries here even Cabell had yet to penetrate. But what also gripped Lang was a sudden existential dread, rooted in the fact that war was not something humankind had invented, but was pervasive throughout the known universe. It brought to mind the rumors he had been hearing, to the effect that General Edwards was already pressing for the construction of an entire *fleet* of warships. According to his camp, the return mission had to recognize a new priority: the idea of peaceful, preventative negotiations was no longer viable— not when war against the Masters was now viewed as a certainty.

Oddly enough, Cabell took no issue with Edwards's demands. It was not so much that he wished to see the Masters of his race obliterated—although he himself would have gladly put to death the cloned body politic they had created—it was his unassailable fear of the Invid.

"Of course I applaud this victory and the freeing of my people," Cabell told him. "But you must believe me when I tell you, Doctor, that the greatest threat to your planet is the Invid. Put aside your sympathy—I know, I saw it in your face. They are not the race they once were; they are homeless now, and *driven*. They will stop at nothing to regain their precious Flowers, and if that matrix exists— they will find it."

Lang wore a sardonic look. "Perhaps it would be better to do nothing—except pray that the Masters find the matrix and leave."

"I fear they will not leave, Doctor. They have all they

need with them, and your world will be nothing but a new battleground."

"So what choice do we have?"

"Defeat them here, Doctor. Exterminate them before you face the Masters."

Lang was aghast. "You're talking about genocide, Cabell."

Cabell shook his head sadly. "No, I am talking about *survival*. Besides," the old man thought to add, "your race seems to have a penchant for that sort of thing."

Rick was among the dozens of VT pilots who had ended up in sick bay. There was no tally of the dead and wounded yet, but the hospital was already overcrowded and shuttles were still bringing up men and women from the moon's surface.

When Lisa first received word of his injuries she thought she might faint; but she was relieved now, knowing that his condition had improved from guarded to good, and that he had been moved out of ICU and into a private room. But she wasn't exactly rushing to his side, and couldn't help but feel somehow vindicated for her earlier remarks. At the same time, she recalled the last visit she had paid Rick in sick bay. It was shortly before the SDF-1 had left Earth for a second time—ordered off by Russo's council—and Khyron's Botoru had been waging a savage attack against the fortress. Rick was badly wounded during a missile barrage Lisa herself had ordered. She remembered how frightened and helpless she had felt that cool Pacific morning, seeing him in the throes of shock and delirium, his head turbaned in gauze and bandages . . . It was a painful memory even now, eight years later, but she was determined not to let it soften the anger that had crept in to replace her initial dismay—an easy enough challenge when she found him sitting up in bed and grinning, well-attended by the nursing staff.

"Here you go, hero," she said, placing a small gift on the sheet, "I brought you something."

Rick unwrapped the package and glanced at the audio disc it contained—a self-help guide that had been a best-seller on Earth and was enjoying an enormous popularity on the fortress. He showed Lisa a confused look. *"The Hand That's Dealt You* . . . What's this supposed to mean?"

Lisa sat on the edge of the bed. "I think it's something you should hear."

Rick put the disc aside and stared at her a moment. "You're still angry."

"I want to know what you intend to do, Rick."

He looked away, down at his bandaged arm. "I'm going to meet with the Council tomorrow."

Lisa couldn't believe what she was hearing, but managed to keep her voice even and controlled. "You're making a big mistake, Rick. Can I talk you out of it?"

He reached for her hand and met her gaze. "No, babe. I know where I belong. I just want you to respect my decision."

She let go of his hand and stood up. "It's not a matter of respect, Rick. Can't you understand that you've picked the worst possible moment to resign? Who else has your experience? This ship is as much yours as anyone's, and Lang is going to need you to supervise the recon—"

"I don't want to hear it."

Lisa huffed at him. "Edwards will be taking over. Doesn't *that* mean anything to you?" Lisa paced away from the bed and whirled around. "You haven't heard the latest, have you?"

"And I don't want to. I'm a pilot."

"You're a disappointment," she said as she left the room.

On another level of the fortress, Jean Grant was crying in her husband's arms; Vince, in his usual fashion, was trying to be strong about it, but there were tears in his eyes. They had just shuttled up from the GMU, their first time offworld in days, and fatigue and intensity finally had had a chance to catch up with them. Perhaps in a last-ditch effort to escape this moment, Jean had tried to run off to sick bay to assist the med teams, but Vince had restrained her. Max and Miriya were present in the couple's spacious cabin.

Max handed them both a drink. "Medicine for melancholy," he said, forcing a smile.

Max, too, wore his share of bandages under his uniform; there had been more than the usual complement of close calls, at least one of which could be traced to his protective attitude toward Rick. Max had suffered some minor burns because of it, but Rick had nearly gotten himself killed. That he saved Rick's life was all that mattered —a secret only he and Miriya shared.

Jean thanked him for the drink and wiped her cheeks with the palms of her hands. "What are we going to do?" she put to all of them.

"We're going to pitch in and make it happen," Vince said, knocking back the drink in one gulp. "It can't take forever to get the generators back in shape."

Max and Miriya traded looks. "Five years," she said.

Jean gasped. "Miriya, no!"

"That's just Lang's first estimate," Max added hurriedly, trying to be helpful. "And I'm sure he's playing it well on the safe side."

"But *five years*, Max . . . The kids . . ."

Vince put a massive arm around his wife's trembling shoulders and quieted her. "They're both better off where they are."

"With war on the way?" Jean's face flushed with anger. "Don't patronize me, any of you!" Distraught, she sighed and apologized.

Miriya said, "Even if it takes five years we'll reach Earth ahead of the Masters. They abandoned Tirol ten years ago, and Cabell's guess is that it will take them another ten."

"Estimates," Jean said. "Is that how we'll explain it to Bowie and Dana—that we guessed wrong in thinking the Masters would be here?"

No one had an answer for her.

"So *this* is all that remains of Tirol's children."

Arms akimbo, Breetai drew himself up to his full Micronized height and made a disappointed sound. All around him Tiresia's humanoid citizenry—the weak and aged fringe who had taken to Tirol's wastes during the Great Transition—were being cared for by med-staff personnel from the GMU, which had been moved from its LZ to an area near the center of the ruined city. Elsewhere, Destroids and Hovertanks patrolled the streets, continuing their search-and-sweep and cordoning off restricted areas, including the Royal Hall's vast circular plaza.

Exedore, who had shuttled down to the surface with members of Lang's Robotech team, heard the anger and frustration in Breetai's words. And he knew that Breetai spoke for all the Zentraedi under his command.

"You would no doubt have preferred a face-to-face encounter with the Masters, Commander."

"I won't deny it." He looked down at his companion. "I feel . . . what is the word, Exedore?"

"*Cheated*, my lord."

Breetai inclined his head knowingly. "Yes. Although . . ."

Exedore raised an eyebrow.

". . . on some level, we failed."

To recapture Zor's ship and return the matrix, Exedore completed. It was the Imperative reasserting its hold, the Masters' cruel imprint. He was tempted to point out that the matrix would only have made it as far as Dolza's hands in any case. But what was the use of contradicting Breetai? Besides, Exedore had more pressing concerns on his mind.

"Commander," he said at last, "have you arrived at a decision yet?"

Breetai grunted. "You have become quite the diplomat, Exedore." He turned to regard Fantoma's sinister crescent in the skies behind him, thinking, *Zarkopolis, where my real past lies buried*. To be returned there after so much space and time . . .

"We will comply with Lang's request."

Exedore smiled. *An even older imperative*. "It was meant to be," he said, eyes fixed on the living remnants of the Masters' fallen empire.

T. R. Edwards studied his reflection, leaning in toward the mirror in his quarters, fingertips playing across the raised and jagged devastation of his face. The scars could easily have been erased by microsurgical techniques, but a *cosmetic* solution was the last thing Edwards desired. In their raw ugliness, they were a constant reminder of the deep-seated injuries spread through the rest of his body and soul—areas no laser scalpel could reach or transform.

He was feverish, and had been so since the incidents in the Royal Hall; it was almost as if his brief contact with the Invid brain had stirred something within him. Beneath the fever's physical haze his thinking was lighting-quick and inspired; his goal was clear, and the path to it well-marked. He realized now that he had been guilty of a kind of reductionist approach to both purpose and destiny. He had convinced himself that Earth was the star—a Ptolemaic sin—when actually the planet was little more than a supporting player in a much grander drama. But he was finally beginning to understand that *there were worlds for the taking*!

He rationalized his failures, however, blaming fate for having kept him Earthbound while the SDF-1 had spent two years of cosmic journeying.

Let Zand and Moran and Leonard play their little games on Earth. Edwards laughed to himself. *And let the Masters arrive to* soften *things up*. In the meantime he would construct the fleet to conquer all of them! It was going to require a good deal of manipulation to wrest the Council from Hunter and Lang's control, but he suddenly felt more than up to the task. Perhaps if Hunter could be fooled into setting off on some secondary mission . . .

Edwards savored the thought. Lang would be preoccupied with overseeing the mining project, Reinhardt was no problem, and the Zentraedi would be offworld. That still left Max Sterling and that troublemaker Wolff, but how difficult could it be to undermine them?

Edwards struck a gleeful, triumphant pose in front of the mirror. "No more demolished man," he said to his reflection. "Let the games begin."

A week went by, then another, and still there was no sign of the Invid. The high command began to wonder if the battle for Tirol hadn't been won after all. With the Masters gone and no trace of the Flowers of Life, the Invid had little use for the world; so perhaps they had simply disregarded it. Cabell spoke of other planets the Invid were thought to occupy—worlds that had been seeded by Zor. Surely those constituted more than enough to satisfy them; and moreover, what quarrel could they possibly have with Earth at this stage of the game?

With all this in mind, a gradual transfer of personnel, stores, and equipment to the surface of Tirol had commenced. Refortified, Tiresia would serve as the RDF's tactical and logistical headquarters. The SDF-3, with a substantially reduced crew and half the VT squadrons, was to remain in stationary orbit, protecting both the moon and the soon-to-be-operative mining colony on Fantoma.

Hope and optimism began to find their way back into the mission once everyone accepted the conditions of the extended stay, and it was only a matter of time before a certain celebratory air took hold. Terrans and Tiresians worked side-by-side clearing away the horrors of the recent past, and the city seemed to rejuvenate. Both sides had known death and suffering at the same alien hands, so there was already a bond of sorts. The Council, hoping to enlarge in this and at the same time take advantage of Earth's New Year's Day, finally scheduled a holiday.

A rousing set from Minmei and Janice accompanied by their newly-formed backup band kicked things off. The superstar of the SDF-1 performed with an enthusiasm she hadn't demonstrated in years, and dug into everyone's collective past to blow the dust off songs like "We Can Win" and "Stagefright," classics for most of the crowd, nostalgia for some. After the set she danced the night away with heroes and rear-echelon execs, but spent most of that time in the embrace of Jonathan Wolff. No one was surprised when the two of them disappeared together halfway through the festivities.

Nor was Dr. Lang surprised to see that his AI creation

had zeroed in on Rem, whom Lang, despite Cabell's claims to the contrary, seemed desperate to accept as Zor incarnate. He had been meaning to urge Janice to move in just that direction—for who knew what secrets Rem and Cabell might be hiding?—but Lang's personal encoding of the android had made that unnecessary: Janice was as attracted to Zor's likeness as Lang was. Cabell, unaware of Janice's laboratory origins, seemed positively delighted by the fact that she and Rem had coupled off; round midnight he was even out on the dance floor executing a Tiresian clogging step that looked to some like an old Geppetto jig straight out of *Pinocchio*.

Elsewhere in the crowd, Jack Baker and Karen Penn were talking; when Vince Grant had rescinded the order that had kept them both confined to quarters, Karen had reversed her own decision never to speak to Jack again.

"Come on, Karen—just one dance," Jack was saying, tailing her as she threaded her way across the floor. "One dance is gonna kill ya?"

Karen stopped short and whirled on him; he brought his hands up expecting a spin kick, and she began to laugh. "I'm talking to you, Jack—isn't that enough?"

"Well, no, dammit, it's *not* enough." Karen was back in motion again. Jack ignored a bit of razzing from friends and set out after her.

"All right," she said, finally. "But just *one*." She held up a finger.

"My choice?"

"Anything you want. Let's just get it over with."

He waited until the band played a long, slow number.

"You gotta admit," he said, holding her, "it was a good ride while it lasted."

She held him at arm's length for a moment, then smiled. "The best . . ."

Not everyone was dancing, however. Or smiling. Years later, in fact, some would say that the "New Year's" celebration showed just how factionalized the Expeditionary mission had become in less than a month out of Earth-space. At the center sat Lang, Exedore, and the Council, joined now by Tirol's unofficial representative, Cabell; while the fringe played host to two discreet groups, Edwards's surly Ghost Riders, and Breetai's Zentraedi, on what would be one of their last nights as Micronized warriors. And separate from any of these groups were certain RDF teams, the Skull Squadron, the Wolff Pack, Grant's GMU contingent.

Rick Hunter, recovered from his wounds, seemed to occupy a middle ground he and Lisa had staked out for themselves. They had been trying hard to make some sense of their dilemma, slowly, sometimes painfully. But at least they were lovers again, back on the honeymoon trail, and confident that things would work themselves out. The Council had yet to rule on Rick's request, and for the time being the topic was shelved.

"Home, sweet home," Rick was telling Lisa. He put his arm around her and motioned with his chin to Tirol's star-studded sky. "We'll have to draw up a new set of constellations."

Lisa rested her head on his shoulder.

"Which way's Earth?"

Lisa pointed. "There—our entire local group."

Rick was silent a moment. "Whaddaya say we dance, Mrs. Hunter?"

"Thought you'd never ask."

They walked hand-in-hand toward the center of the floor, and were just into their first step when the music came to an abrupt stop. Murmurs swept through the crowd and everyone turned to the stage. Dr. Lang was at a mike stand, apologizing for the interruption.

"Listen to me, everyone," he was saying. "We have just received a dispatch from the SDF-3. An unidentified ship has just entered the Valivarre system. It is decelerating and on a probable course for Tirol. General Reinhardt has put the fortress on high alert, and suggests that we do the same. Skull and Ghost Squadrons are ordered to report to the shuttle-launch facilities at once. CD personnel are to report to their unit commanders immediately. Admiral Hayes and Admiral Hunter—"

"Lisa, come on," Rick shouted, tugging at her arm.

She resisted, hoping she would wake from this, so they could continue their dance—

"Come on!" Rick was repeating . . .

The war had come between them again!

The following chapter is a sneak preview of DARK DEBUT—Book II in the SENTINELS saga.

■ ■ ■ ■ ■ ■ ■ ■ ■ ■ ■ ■ ■ ■ ■ ■ ■ ■

CHAPTER
ONE

All I have learned of the Shapings of the Protoculture tell me that it does not work randomly, that there is a grand design or scheme. I feel that we have been brought here, kept here, for some reason.

Yet, what purpose can there be in SDF-3's being stranded here on Tirol for perhaps as long as five years? And during that time will the Robotech Masters be pursuing their search for Earth?

Because many tempers are short, I do not mention the Shaping; I'm a little too long in the tooth, I fear, for hand-to-hand confrontations with homesick, frightened, and frustrated REF fighters.

Dr. Emil Lang's Personal journal of the SDF-3 Mission

O N CAPTURED TIROL, AFTER A FIERCE BATTLE, THE Humans and their Zentraedi allies—the Robotech Expeditionary Force—licked their wounds, then decided it was time to mark the occasion of their triumph. It was, as nearly as they could calculate, New Year's Eve.

But far out near the edge of Tirol's system, a newcomer appeared—a massive space-going battleship, closing in on the war-torn, planet-size moon.

Our first victory celebration, young Susan Graham exulted. *What a wonderful party!* She was just shy of sixteen, and to her it was the most romantic evening in human history.

She was struggling to load a bulky cassette into her sound-vid recorder while scurrying around to get a better angle at Admirals Rick Hunter and Lisa Hayes Hunter. They had just stood up, in full-dress uniforms, clasping white-gloved hands, apparently about to dance. There had been rumors that the relationship between the two senior officers of the Robotech Expeditionary Force was on shaky ground, but for the moment at least, they seemed altogether in love.

Sue let out a short, romantic sigh and envied Lisa Hunter. Then her thoughts returned to the cassette which she was tapping with the heel of her hand. A lowly student-trainee, Sue had to make do with whatever equipment she could find at the G-5 Public Information shop, Psyops, Morale or wherever.

At last the cassette was in place, and she began to move toward her quarry.

In Tiresia, the planet-moon's shattered capital city, the Royal Hall was aglow. The improvised lighting and decorations reemphasized the vast, almost endless size of the place.

The lush ballroom music remained slow—something from Strauss, Karen Penn thought; something even Jack Baker could handle. As she had expected, he asked her to waltz a second time.

And he wasn't too bad at it. The speed and reflexes that made him such a good Veritech pilot—*almost as good as I am*, she thought—made him a passable dancer. Still, she maintained her aloof air, gliding flawlessly, making him seem clumsy by comparison; otherwise, that maddening brashness of his would surface again at any second.

They were about the same height, five-ten or so, he redheaded and freckled and frenetic, she honey-blonde and smooth-skinned and model-gorgeous, and long since tired of panting male attention. Jack had turned eighteen two months ago; Karen would celebrate her majority in three more weeks.

They were like oil and water, cats and dogs, Unseducible Object and Irrepressible Force, ever since they had met. But they had also been battle-comrades, and now they swayed as the music swelled, and somehow their friendly antagonism was put aside, at least for the moment.

The deepspace dreadnought was a bewildering, almost slapdash length of components: different technologies, different philosophies of design, even different stages of scientific awareness, showed in the contrasts among its various modules. From it, scores of disparate weapons bristled and many kinds of sensors probed.

With Tirol before it, the motley battle-wagon went on combat alert.

On the outer rim of the ballroom, members of General Edwards's Ghost Squadron and Colonel Wolff's Wolff Pack traded hostile looks, but refrained from any overt clashes; Admiral Lisa Hunter's warnings, and her promises of retribution, had been very specific on that point.

Edwards was there, a haughty, splendidly military figure, his sardonic handsomeness marred by the half cowl that covered the right half of his head.

Per Lisa's confidential order, Vince Grant and his Ground Mobile Unit people were keeping an eye on the rivals, ready to break up any scuffles. So far things seemed to be peaceful—nothing more than a bit of glowering and boasting.

Hanging in orbit over the war-torn ruin of Tirol, Super

Dimensional Fortress Three registered the rapid approach of the unidentified battleship.

SDF-3 had been tardy in detecting the newcomer; the Earth warship's systems had been damaged in the ferocious engagement that had destroyed her spacefold apparatus, and some systems were still functioning far short of peak efficiency.

But she had spotted the possible adversary now. Following procedure, SDF-3 went to battle stations, and communications personnel rushed to open downlinks with the contingent on Tirol's surface.

Perhaps the strangest pair at the celebration were Janice Em, the lovely and enigmatic singer, and Rem, assistant to the Tiresian scientist Cabell.

Janice was Dr. Lang's creation, an android, an Artificial Person, though she was unaware of it. Rem was the clone of the original Zor, the discoverer of Protoculture, creator of miracles and holocausts, and also unaware of it.

Lang shook his head and reminded himself that the Shapings of the Protoculture were not to be defied. He was really quite happy that the two were drawn together.

He turned to Cabell, the ancient lone-survivor of the scientists of Tirol.

What was once the gorgeous cityscape of Tiresia, and magnificent gardens surrounding the Royal Hall, was now only a blasted wasteland.

Above was a jade-green crescent of Fantoma, the massive planet that Tirol circled. Its alien beauty hid the ugliness that Lynn-Minmei knew to be there in the light of Valivarre, the system's primary. The green Fantoma-light cast a spell with magic all its own. How could the scene of so much death and suffering be so unspeakably beautiful?

She shivered a bit, and Colonel Jonathan Wolff slipped his arm around her. Minmei could feel from the way he had moved closer that he wanted to kiss her; she wasn't sure whether she felt the same or not.

He was the debonair, tigerishly brave, good-looking Alpha-Wolf of the Wolff Pack—and had rescued her from certain death, melodramatic as it might sound to others. Still, there was a danger in love; she had learned that, not once but several times now.

Wolff could see what was running through Minmei's thoughts. He feasted his eyes on her, hungered for her. The Big, Bad Wolff, indeed—an expression he had never liked.

Only this time, the Big Bad was bewitched, and helpless. She was the blue-eyed, black-haired gamine whose voice and guileless charm had been the key to Human victory in the Robotech War. She was the child-woman who had, unknowingly, tormented him with fantasies he could not exorcize by day, and with erotic fever-dreams by night.

She hadn't moved from the circle of his arm; she looked at him, eyes wide as those of a startled doe. Wolff leaned closer, lips parting.

I love her so much, Rick thought, as he and Lisa went to join the dancing. His wife's waist was supple under his gloved hand; her eyes shone with fondness. He felt himself breaking into a languorous smile, and she beamed at him.

I can't live without her, he knew. *All these problems between us—we'll find some way to deal with them. Because otherwise life's not worth living.*

The music had just begun when it stopped again, raggedly, as Dr. Lang quieted people from the mike stand. The ship's orchestra's conductor stood to one side, looking peeved but apprehensive.

Everyone there had already served in war. Something in side them anticipated the words. "Unidentified ship... course for Tirol... Skull and Ghost Squadrons... Admiral Hayes and Admiral Hunter..."

The war's come between us again.

Rick started off in a dash, but stopped before he had gone three steps, realizing his wife was no longer with him. Fortunately, in all the confusion, only one person noticed.

He looked back and saw Lisa waiting there, head erect, watching him. He realized he had reacted with a fighter jock's reflexes, the headlong run of a hot-scramble.

It was the argument they had been having for days, for weeks now—tersely, in quick exchanges, by day; wearily, taxing the limits of their patience with one another, by night. Rick was a pilot, and had come to the conclusion that he couldn't be—*shouldn't* be—anything else. Lisa insisted that his job now was to command, to oversee Flight Group ops. He was to do the job he had been chosen to do because nobody else could do it.

Rick saw nothing but confidence in his wife's eyes as she looked at him, her chin held high—that, and a proud set to her features.

Sue Graham, wielding her aud-vid recorder, had caught the whole thing, the momentary lapse in protocol, in confidence—in love. Now, she rewound the tape a bit, so that the sight of Rick Hunter dashing off from his wife would be obliterated, and began recording over it.

Just as people were turning to the Admirals-Hunter, Rick stepped closer to Lisa. In that time, conversation and noise died away, and the Royal Hall itself, weighted by its eons of history and haunting events, seemed to be listening, evaluating. Rick's high dress boots clacked on an alien floor that shone like a black mirror.

He offered her his arm, formal and meticulously correct, inclining his head to her. "Madam?"

She did a shallow military curtsy, supple in her dress-uniform skirt, and laid her hand on his forearm. The whole room was listening and watching; Rick and Lisa had reminded everyone what the REF was, and what was expected of it.

"Orders, Admiral?" Rick asked his wife crisply, loudly, in his role as second-ranking-officer-present. By speaking those words, he officially ended the ball and put everyone on notice that they were on duty.

Lisa, suddenly their rock, gazed about at them. She didn't have to raise her voice very much to be heard. "You all know what to do—ladies, gentlemen.

"We will treat this as a red alert. SDF-3 will stand to General Quarters. GMU and other ground units report to combat stations; all designated personnel will return to the Dimensional Fortress."

Already, there was movement as people strode or hurried to their duties. But no one was running, Lisa had given them back their center.

"Fire control and combat operations officers will ensure that no provocative or hostile acts are committed," she said in a sharp voice. "I will remind you that we are *still* on a *diplomatic mission*.

"Carry on."

Men and women were moving purposefully, the yawning hall quickly clearing. Lisa turned to an aide, a commo officer. "My respects to the Plenipotentiary Council, and would they be so gracious as to convene a meeting immediately upon my return to SDF-3."

The aide disappeared; Lisa turned to Rick. "If you please?"

Rick, his wife on his arm, turned toward the shuttle

grounding area. REF personnel made way for them. Rick let Lisa set the pace: businesslike, but not frantic.

When the shuttle was arrowing up through Tirol's atmosphere for SDF-3 rendezvous, the two studied preliminary reports while staff officers ran analyses and more data poured in. Rick paused for a moment to look at his wife, as she meditated over the most recent updates.

He covered her hand with his for a moment; squeezed it. "We owe each other a waltz, Lisa."

She gave him a quick, loving smile, squeezing his hand back. Then she turned to issue more orders to her staff.

To Rem, the Humans and their REF mission had been bewildering from the beginning, but never more so than now.

With this news of a unidentified warship, he and his mentor Cabell—who had been a father to him, really, and more than a father—were chivvied toward the shuttle touchdown area, to await their turn to be lifted up to the SDF-3. Their preference in the matter wasn't asked; they were an important—perhaps crucial—military intelligence resource now, even though they were just as mystified as anybody else.

There were confused snatches of conversation and fragments of scenes as Rem guided Cabell along in the general milling.

There were the two young cadets Rem had come to know as Karen Penn and Jack Baker. They had been pressed into service as crowd controllers and expediters of the evacuation. Jack kept trying to catch Karen's eye and call some sort of jest or other; she just spared him the occasional withering glance and concentrated on her duties

Rem couldn't blame her. What could be funny about a

situation like this? Was Jack psychologically malfunctional?

Then there was the singer, Minmei, Janice Em's partner, possessed of a voice so moving that it defied logic, and a face and form of unsettling appeal. The one they called Colonel Wolff seemed to be trying to usher her along, seemed to be proprietary toward her, but she wasn't having any of it. In fact, it appeared that she was about to burst into that startling and alarming human physiological aberration called *tears*.

The Ghost and Skull and GMU teams were cooperating like a mindlinked triumverate, though Rem had seen them ready to come to blows only a short time before.

He looked about for Janice Em, Minmei's partner and harmony and, in some measure, alter ego, but couldn't see her. She had been with Lang only moments before, but now Lang was gone, too. Rem tried to push troubling thoughts from his mind, such as the rumors that were rife about Lang and Janice. Lang was supposed to be like an uncle to her, though some said he was "much more."

But *what*? Rem barely understood the concept "uncle," and had no idea what "much more" might mean. Yet his cheeks flushed, and he felt a puzzling rage when he thought of Jan having some nebulous relationship to Lang that would make the old Human scientist more important to her than, than . . .

Then all at once Rem and Cabell were being rushed into a shuttle, and a sliding hatch cut off the haunted nighttime view of ruined Tiresia.

ABOUT THE AUTHOR

Jack McKinney has been a psychiatric aide, fusion-rock guitarist and session man, worldwide wilderness guide, and "consultant" to the U.S. Military in Southeast Asia (although they had to draft him for that).

His numerous other works of mainstream and science fiction—novels, radio and television scripts—have been written under various pseudonyms.

He currently resides in Ubud, on the Indonesian island of Bali.

THE EPIC SAGA CONTINUES

ROBOTECH

by
JACK McKINNEY

Available at your bookstore or use this coupon.

____ DOOMSDAY #6	34139-2	$2.95
____ SOUTHERN CROSS #7	34140-6	$2.95
____ METAL FIRE #8	34141-4	$2.95
____ THE FINAL NIGHTMARE #9	34142-2	$2.95
____ INVID INVASION #10	34143-0	$2.95
____ METAMORPHOSOS #11	34144-9	$2.95
____ SYMPHONY OF LIGHT #12	345-34145-7	$2.95

BB BALLANTINE MAIL SALES
Dept. TA, 201 E. 50th St., New York, N.Y. 10022

Please send me the BALLANTINE or DEL REY BOOKS I have checked
above. I am enclosing $....................(add 50¢ per copy to cover postage
and handling). Send check or money order—no cash or C.O.D.'s please.
Prices and numbers are subject to change without notice. Valid in U.S.
only. All orders are subject to availablility of books.

Name_____

Address_____

City_____ State_____ Zip Code_____

Allow at least 4 weeks for delivery.